THE CLASSIC COLLECTION SERIES

The Classic Collection series' undergirding philosophy is:

• The series should feature books for the entire family, not just one age group.

• The books should lend themselves to being read aloud, thus encouraging families to bring back a time-honored—but, in today's TV-dominated society, almost lost—tradition of the family hour, when the entire family spent time together.

• The books should espouse Judeo-Christian values.

• Generally speaking, the books should be selected from the ranks of those that have stood the test of time: Generations have come and gone, but these books are still loved, still relevant, still speak to the heart.

• The books should as often as possible incorporate early woodcut illustrations or similar art. In other words, the books in this series are intended to be *keepers*, the kind given as heirloom gifts, treasured from generation to generation.

• Each book will include a modest biography of the author, a bibliography of his or her other works, and background material to help the reader understand how a particular book (and author) evolved.

• Finally, if a book is to become real, and fully understood, it must be discussed—hence discussion questions, general and chapter-specific, have been added in an afterword.

As much as possible, we have tried to respect the sanctity of a text. But where a given book is generations, and sometimes centuries, old, editing is almost essential. It is amazing to see how many words still in use today have acquired new meanings and lost old ones. The difficulty for an editor is securing a close enough synonym so that the meaning is unchanged, yet finding a substitute word that would have been in existence when the book was originally published. Substitutions are especially needed where, over the years, words have acquired negative or sexual connotations. In some cases, words have been changed simply because no dictionary short of a million-word unabridged carries them anymore!

It is both an honor and a privilege to have our series welcomed into your home. It is our earnest and prayerful intent that each of the books chosen will significantly enrich your life and that of your family: that it will provide new insights; emotional, intellectual, and spiritual growth; and increased empathy with, and charity toward, others, particularly those viewed as "different."

A Word to Parents

The books in the Classic Collection series have been selected because they are among the finest literary works in history. However, you should be aware that some content might not be suitable for all ages, so we recommend you review the material before sharing it with your family.

Mr. Fezziwig's Ball

A CHRISTMAS CAROL
In Prose
A Ghost Story of Christmas
by
CHARLES DICKENS

with an Introduction and Afterword by
JOE L. WHEELER, PH.D.

PUBLISHING
Colorado Springs, Colorado

A CHRISTMAS CAROL

Copyright © 1997 by Joseph L. Wheeler and Focus on the Family
All rights reserved. International copyright secured.

ISBN 1-56179-592-5

Classic Collection series #4/Dickens series #1

Published by Focus on the Family Publishing, Colorado Springs, CO 80995

Distributed in the U.S.A. and Canada by Word Books, Dallas, Texas

No part of this publication may be reproduced, stored in a retrieval system, or transmitted in a
form or by any means—electronic, mechanical, photocopy, recording, or otherwise—without
prior permission of the publisher.

Illustrations by John Leech. From the 1843 first edition published by Chapman and Hall, London
The four color plates by John Leech for *A Christmas Carol* have been reproduced with the
permission of Michael Patrick Hearn from his book *The Annotated Christmas Carol* (New Yor
Clarkson N. Potter, Inc., 1976). Copyright© 1976 by Michael Patrick Hearn.

The author is represented by the literary agency of Alive Communications, 1465 Kelly Johnson
Blvd., Suite 320, Colorado Springs, CO 80920.

Focus on the Family books are available at special quantity discounts when purchased in bulk
corporations, organizations, churches, or groups. Special imprints, messages, and excerpts can b
produced to meet your needs. For more information, contact: Sales Dept., Focus on the Family
Publishing, 8605 Explorer Dr., Colorado Springs, CO 80920; or phone (719) 531-3400.

Editor: Michele A. Kendall
Cover Design: Bradley L. Lind
Cover Illustration: Clint Hansen

Printed in the United States of America

97 98 99 00 01 02 03/10 9 8 7 6 5 4 3 2

PREFACE

I have endeavored in this
Ghostly little book to raise the
Ghost of an Idea which shall
not put my readers out of
humor with themselves, with
each other, with the season,
or with me. May it haunt their
house pleasantly, and no one
wish to lay* it.

Their faithful Friend and Servant,

C.D.

December 1843

---

*Prevent.

TABLE OF CONTENTS

List of Illustrations..ix

Introduction — Scrooge in the Crossroads xi

Stave One — Marley's Ghost..................................1

Stave Two — The First of the Three Spirits 21

Stave Three — The Second of the Three Spirits.................41

Stave Four — The Last of the Spirits 67

Stave Five — The End of It 85

Afterword: Discussion with Professor Wheeler......95

LIST OF ILLUSTRATIONS

Mr. Fezziwig's Ball ....Frontispiece

Marley's Ghost 14

Scrooge's Lookout...17

The Extinguisher 38

Scrooge's Third Visitor....................................44

Ignorance and Want.......................................63

The Last of the Spirits.....................................77

The End of It...91

SCROOGE IN THE CROSSROADS

I cannot remember when I first heard it read, nor when I first read it myself, nor when I first experienced it on film, nor even when it first engulfed me as live drama. I only know that looking back through life, somehow *A Christmas Carol* was always there.

In the century and a half since *A Christmas Carol* was published in 1843, we have come to take it for granted: We just accept it as if it had always been with us—like the Wise Men, crèches, and holly. What would the world be like without Scrooge, Marley, the Cratchits, the Three Ghosts, "Bah! Humbug!" and Tiny Tim? Well, in 1842, none of them existed.

What was the year 1843 like for Charles Dickens, anyway? Simply put, it was not good. Let me explain.

As we'll see in the author biography, Dickens endured a tough childhood. Then, at the age of twenty-five, he was catapulted to the top of his world. It is always dangerous to soar too high too young: It usually results in a strong case of hubris—unless the twenty-five-year-old is strong and wise beyond his years; unless he realizes, with Nebuchadnezzar, how quickly the God who giveth can become the God who taketh away. In other words, today's success is already unrealizingly sowing the seeds of its own destruction. This was true with Dickens. He had assumed that he had become great by his own efforts—by the sheer brilliance of his mind and force of his will.

Perhaps a baseball analogy would help. In 1836, Dickens stepped up to the plate and hit *Boz* out of the park. Next, he hit *Pickwick* out of the park. Then *Oliver Twist,* then *Nickleby,* then *The Old Curiosity Shop;* and then *Barnaby Rudge,* which just cleared the outer wall. Then came his ill-fated trip to the United States, and when his bat made contact with *American Notes,* he hit only a bloop single, not realizing that he now had a hairline crack in the bat. *American Notes* was followed by *Martin Chuzzlewit*—and with it, he broke his bat.

For the first time in seven years, Dickens was in trouble. It all began because the Americans refused to pay him his due royalties, which made Dickens angry. Because of his fame, he assumed, mistakenly, that he could say anything he wanted when he traveled to the late great colony of America, so he decided to tell them what he thought of their cheapness. To put his condition in the modern vernacular, he had an attitude problem. Even his countrymen felt he had gone too far.

The result: The golden faucet that had gushed its riches upon Dickens for almost seven years slowed its flow so much that he wondered if perhaps his well was going dry. What if people would no longer buy his books?

Never a humble man, Dickens always knew, to a penny, the value of his gifts. At least, he *thought* he had before 1842. Now, he wasn't so sure anymore.

What could he write that would improve his fortunes and help bring back his fickle public? It had to be something he could write quickly, not just another two-year book serialization. So the idea for *A Christmas Carol* came to him (see biography). For a month and a half, Dickens immersed himself in the world of Scrooge. In the process, he gradually became aware that, somewhere along the way, he had become a Scrooge himself: He had felt so secure in his gifts that he assumed he no longer needed other people—that he no longer needed to care (not just abstractly, but one-on-one) about them.

In the course of writing the story of Scrooge, Dickens was able to pull himself back from the brink and realize his need for others. He began to wonder if he had ever really known who he was. And could he ever really know without going backward in time?

The answers to those questions were a long time in coming, but *A Christmas Carol* was the first step. Dickens learned something else during the writing of this little book: He learned about the difference between writing a lean, cohesive book (written all at once) and writing the usually episodic, rambly serialization.

As a result of this no man's land between the overconfidence of his youth and the social conscience of his maturity, Dickens was able to make it through the rest of his life without being destroyed by pride. He found out things about himself that stripped away some of his arrogance; and sorrow would rock him on his heels again and again.

So it came to pass that in the last quarter of Dickens's life, in his 450 public readings (an average of one performance every twelve days for fifteen years), the story of Scrooge became as indispensable as singing the national anthem at a big league baseball game. And as Dickens's life drew to a close, a higher percentage of each evening's performance was devoted to *A Christmas Carol* and its lesson of agape love.

It is no hyperbole to say that without this one little book, the life of Charles Dickens most likely would have been very different. In a very real sense, then, we may validly say that the *Christmas Carol* characters conceived by this author ended up taking him on a journey that would last a lifetime.

It is our privilege to be invited along. Welcome to the timeless world of *A Christmas Carol.*

ABOUT THE INTRODUCTION

For decades, one of the few absolutes in my literature classes has been this: *Never read the introduction before reading the book!* Those who ignored my thundering admonition lived to regret their disobedience. Downcast, they would come to me and say, "Dr. Wheeler, I confess that I read the introduction first, and it wrecked the book for me. I couldn't enjoy the story, because all the way through I saw it through someone *else's* eyes. I don't agree with the editor on certain points, but those conclusions are in my head, and now I don't know *what* I think!"

Given that God never created a human clone, no two of us will ever perceive reality in exactly the same way—and no two of us ever should! Therefore, no matter how educated, polished, brilliant, insightful, or eloquent the teacher might be, don't ever permit that person to tell you how to think or respond, for that is a violation of the most sacred thing God gives us—our individuality.

My solution to the introduction problem was to split it in two: an introduction, to whet the appetite for, and enrich the reading of, the book; and an afterword, to generate discussion and debate *after* the reader has arrived at his or her own conclusions about the book and is ready to challenge my (the teacher's) perceptions.

MOVIE HISTORY

Year: 1938—*A Christmas Carol,* MGM, black-and-white and colorized, 69 min.
Cast: Reginald Owen, Gene Lockhart, Kathleen Lockhart, Terence Kilburne, Leo G. Carroll, Lynne Carver, Ann Rutherford, Barry Mackay, June Lockhart (screen debut)
Director: Edwin L. Marin

Year: 1951—*A Christmas Carol,* or, *Scrooge* (British), black-and-white and colorized, 86 min.
Cast: Alastair Sim, Kathleen Harrison, Jack Warner, Michael Hordern, Patrick Macnee, Mervyn Johns, Hermione Baddeley, Clifford Mollison, George Cole, Carol Marsh, Miles Malleson, Ernest Thesiger, Hattie Jacques, Peter Bull, Hugh Dempster
Director: Brian Desmond Hurst
Screenplay: Noel Langley
Composer: Richard Addinsell

Year: 1954—*A Christmas Carol* (musical), black-and-white, 54 min.
Cast: Frederic March, Basil Rathbone, Ray Middleton, Bob Sweeney, Christopher Cook

Year: 1984—*A Christmas Carol,* color, 100 min.; filmed in Shrewsbury, England
Cast: George C. Scott, Nigel Davenport, Frank Finlay, Edward Woodward, Lucy Gutteridge, Angela Pleasence, Roger Rees, David Warner, Susannah York, Anthony Walters
Director: Clive Donner
Screenplay: Roger O. Hirson

ABOUT THE AUTHOR

Though I have studied and taught Charles Dickens throughout my teaching career, this is the first time I have dug so deeply into the various strata of his life. Two definitive biographies gave me bedrock to build on: Edgar Johnson's monumental *Charles Dickens: His Tragedy and Triumph* (New York: Viking Press, 1977; first edition, 1952); and Fred Kaplan's powerful *Dickens: A Biography* (New York: William Morrow & Company, 1988). A wealth of additional material came from E.W.F. Tomlin's engrossing *Charles Dickens:*

A Centennial Volume (New York: Simon & Schuster, 1970); Jane R. Cohen's *Charles Dickens and His Original Illustrators* (Columbus: Ohio State University Press, 1980); and Michael Patrick Hearn's splendid *The Annotated Christmas Carol* (New York: Clarkson N. Potter, 1976)—Mr. Hearn has kindly given me permission to enrich this edition by the treasure trove of information appearing in the footnotes. Perhaps the ultimate dictionary of our time, invaluable for words no longer in use, is *The Compact Edition of the Oxford English Dictionary* (New York and Glasgow: Oxford University Press, 1973). The 1946 edition of the *Encyclopedia Britannica* provided me with G. K. Chesterton's succinctly written biographical synthesis of Dickens's life and works. For additional enjoyment and insights, I encourage you to search out these books and read them in their entirety.

— — —

There can never be another Dickens. . . . If a novelist of similar genius appeared tomorrow, we could safely prophesy he would never arrive at the height of popularity Dickens held for thirty years. The Victorians wanted Dickens novels as nobody these days really wants anybody's novels. They were the great family entertainment, with something for everybody. (J. B. Priestly in Tomlin, p. 27)

The Victorian age was a different world than the one we live in today. First of all, print was king. Books and magazines were as exciting to those living a century and a half ago as the cinema is to us today—more so, in fact, for we have quickly become jaded to a medium that bombards us so incessantly, that gives us no peace, no blessed silence in which to think and reflect.

But not so then. The home was still central to life, and divorce was incredibly rare. Large families were the norm; they had to be, for of six children, if only two survived to adulthood, that would barely replace the mother and father, much less enable the population to grow. Since so few children received any education, and since so many children entered the workforce at such an early age (six to twelve being the norm among poorer families), large families did not cost as much, by percentage of family income, as they do today.

Fathers ruled supreme, and their word was law—as often as not, even after the children had grown up. This was especially true with the daughters: Often, a father would selfishly refuse to let a daughter marry, keeping her at home as cheap labor for life and guaranteeing him health care in old age.

There was no central heat or central air, so during the winter everyone congregated around the fireplace or the kitchen stove; and during the summer they'd find the coolest room in the house (high ceilings resulted in relative coolness on floor level, and cross-ventilating windows helped to cool the house as well). With no televisions, no CD-ROMs, no VCRs, no videos, no cinemas, no radios even, what did people do back then? They read—and created their own entertainment.

Normally, they weren't interested in a "quick read," for the evenings were long. And they created their own inner imagery, for illustrations were few. Let me give you a fun assignment: Start your own archaeological expedition by searching out old magazines (the easiest to find are bound volumes in antique stores) and see how far back you can go. What you will find is that, before 1860, magazines carried few illustrations, and the illustrations that did appear were usually crude, simplistic, or stereotyped. It's almost as if there's a huge wall separating the years before 1860 from the years after that date. Do a similar search with full-length books. Your conclusions will be the same. Thus, at that time in history, the words themselves had to provide not only the story line but also the visual effects.

Furthermore, since full-length, bound books were expensive, few people could afford to buy them; hence, the need for story serializations that appeared weekly, every other week, or monthly (the original soap operas). Most of Dickens's books were part of this tradition, being hawked on street corners, sold in bookstores, or included in magazines (which were sold in the same way). Once you know this fact about early nineteenth-century publishing, you will understand a lot about the books themselves. For instance, they all have roller-coaster story lines. Each chapter is already in motion and includes deep plunges and neck-jarring turns; and each chapter ends on a high summit looking down into an abyss—that was to make sure you would toss and turn all week, waiting for the next installment.

The whole family—usually six to twelve children, mother, father, and other relatives—would gather around on an evening, and the stories would be read aloud, often being passed from one reader to the next. Thus each story became an integral part of the family psyche and memories—not just the hearing or reading of them, but also the individualized and collective responses to certain passages.

Further reinforcement came later as families put on their own dramatic skits, adding yet another dimension to the story lines. Sadly, today the entire process of passing on a story has degenerated to spoon-feeding pabulum to youngsters: Everything is so predigested and prepackaged that all one has to do is flop down on a couch, half-asleep, and let a given story wash over and into you, punctuated by potty-break commercials.

Given this difference between the nineteenth century and the late twentieth, it is small wonder that, during Dickens's time, families gathered authors into their hearts in ways unthinkable today, considering them greater than royalty or heads of state. Authors were the superstars of their age.

And for his time, Dickens was the number one box-office draw—both in the British Empire and in the United States.

Let's see how all of this came to be.

A Strange Sort of Pot to Grow In

The row house in which Charles John Huffam Dickens was born on February 7, 1812, still stands: 387 Mile End Terrace, Landport, Portsea, not far from London. Like most of the homes the boy was to know, it proved to be but a way station to something else. Before he was five months old, the family moved again, to something cheaper.

It was a most undistinguished family into which Dickens was born—none of them known to memory had ever done much to crow about. His mother, Elizabeth Barrow, born in 1788, was slim, dark-haired, hazel-eyed, pretty, and loved to dance; in fact, on the night her second child was born, she attended a ball. That attitude of carelessness and devotion to self would remain unchanged through the years. Nevertheless, she was cheerful, sweet-tempered, and well-educated for the time. A remarkable mimic, she had a keen sense of the ridiculous, which she would have much need of, given that she was married to John Dickens.

John Dickens, born in 1785, was an eternal optimist, always perceiving his glass of life as half-full rather than half-empty. He took seriously his job as clerk in the navy pay office, which paid £176 a year. Generous, cheerful, kind, warm-hearted, and hospitable—he loved to entertain—John had one flaw: His outgo was invariably more than his income. All his life, he borrowed from tomorrow to pay for today. His son was to re-create him in many forms—to Chesterton, John Dickens was halfway between Micawber and Dorrit: "a man of wavering and unstable status, partly by his misfortunes and partly by his fault" (*Britannica* VII, p. 331). Ostensibly genteel, John was a wondrous talker, always seeming to be more than he was—"magnilo-quent," according to Johnson. In that sense, David Copperfield's Micawber is his portrait, etched in undying colors.

The Dickens family would always be on the move. To John and Elizabeth, it was just the way things were. Both took life as it came, never getting very upset when troubles deluged them. Their laughter always burbled through the rain.

Young Charles was to know only one short period of relative tranquility and stability: When he was five, his father was transferred to the naval yards in Chatham, a shipbuilding town that was even then becoming part of the cathedral city of Rochester. Besides his older sister, Fanny, Charles had a baby sister, Letitia. John, now earning £300 a year, moved into a three-story brick house (also part of a row-house complex) on Ordnance Terrace, overlooking the river Medway. There were small front and back gardens, a couple of hawthorn trees to climb, and fields nearby that filled with wildflowers in the spring.

The Dickenses were well enough off to afford two servants: Jane Bonny and Mary Weller. The latter, Charles never forgot because of the horrifying stories she told him at night. "One of these gory narratives concerned a certain Captain Murderer who slaughtered his successive wives, baked them in meat pies, ate them, and picked their bones" (Johnson, p. 17). Another horrific tale had to do with a Faustian figure who sold himself to the devil and ended up in a nightmare world haunted by rats. Needless to say, these stories were anything but conducive to sleep: "Little Charles would lie in bed rigid with terror" (Johnson, p. 18). Perhaps because of Mary Weller's gruesome stories, early on Charles became obsessed with cannibalism—an interest he never lost, even after he grew up.

Charles learned to read at his mother's knee, and from then on, he read voraciously. He and Fanny attended a dame school for a time; the grim old woman who ran the school, Charles would remember all his life, later portraying her as the Mrs. Pipchin who would help to make Paul Dombey's life so miserable.

It was in Chatham that Charles first fell in love. Next door lived two children, George and Lucy Stroughill. Charles would remember Lucy all his life as a "peach-faced creature with a blue sash" (Johnson, p. 19).

Fanny and Charles enjoyed singing comic songs together, and the proud father would often hoist his son onto the table and have him entertain guests in his high childish treble. Charles would also sing sea duets with Fanny while both stood on the dining room table.

Sometimes in life, apparently simple acts have far-reaching results. Oftentimes Charles and his father would walk together on the Gravesend to Rochester road; as they'd cross the Rochester Bridge, up ahead like a fairyland palace on top of Gad's Hill would rise a brick Georgian mansion, with bow windows and a small white bell turret. One day his father, noting a look of dreamy longing on his son's face, said, "If you are very prospering, and work very hard, you may someday come to live in it" (Johnson, p. 11). Charles, a veteran of cramped living quarters, considered that statement in partial disbelief and in partial hope, then stored away the moment among the rest of his young dreams. Through the long years ahead, the glow of that one vision of Gad's Hill Place would remain in his mind as a beacon of the possible.

Great windjammer battleships riding proudly at anchor in the Chatham Naval Yard, the narrow streets climbing up to towering Rochester Cathedral, the romantic ruins of a once great castle, the verdant hills of Kent, and the gilded river Medway meandering its way down to the English Channel across from France . . . these images represented Dickens's personal Eden, the sanctuary to which he could retreat when his world darkened. It was a time when he felt secure and loved.

The streets of Chatham—filled as they were with jostling tradesmen, shopping women, convict laborers, sailors, and soldiers—always excited Dickens. Downriver a ways great ship hulks housed prisoners when they were not working. When one of them escaped, guns were fired, warning everyone to lock their doors. But it was the river that most filled young Charles's dreams. Hour after hour, he would wander down its banks, listening to the tide come in and go out, watching the boats, barges, and ships as he daydreamed.

Because the whole family was musical and loved drama, their home life was filled with both. Fanny was already taking piano and voice lessons, preparing for a musical career. The theater, in those pre-media days, was everywhere. But the first escape into that world that Charles could remember was "the delights—the ten thousand million delights of a pantomime . . . [to] which a long row of small boys, with frills as white as they could be washed, and hands as clean as they would come, were taken to behold the glories. . . . What mattered it that the stage was three yards wide, and four deep? We never saw it. We had no eyes, ears or corporeal sense, but for the pantomime" (Kaplan, p. 27). He was seven when he first heard the great Grimaldi perform in London.

To his home Charles brought the theater—charades, pantomimes, comedies, melodrama, magic-lantern shows. He could direct, as well as act in, everything. He could even write his own dramas. But in the famed Rochester

Theatre Royale, he saw the great actors of the age—including the tragedian Edmund Kean and the comedian Charles Matthews—tread the boards. It was in this theater that Charles first shuddered at the evil of Richard III and the witches in *Macbeth*. Oliver Goldsmith and William Shakespeare were his two theatrical idols.

And his stagestruck father, on their long walks together, would thunder out or whisper memorable lines from the great dramas—all of which the child absorbed as parched ground does drops of rain.

At home, Charles had long since graduated from "Jack and the Bean Stalk," "The Yellow Dwarf," "Robin Hood," "Red Riding Hood" and "Valentine and Orson" to his parents' books: *Roderick Random, Peregrine Pickle, Humphrey Clinker, Tom Jones, Don Quixote, Gil Blas,* and *Robinson Crusoe.* Remembering years later, he wrote,

> When I think of it, the picture always arises in my mind of a summer evening, the boys at play in the churchyard and I sitting on my bed, reading as if for life. Every barn in the neighborhood, every stone in the church, and every foot of the churchyard, had some association of its own, in my mind, connected with these books, and stood for some locality made famous in them. I have seen Tom Pipes go climbing up the church steeple; I have watched Strap, with the knapsack on his back, stopping to rest upon the wicket-gate; and I know that Commodore Trinnion held that club with Mr. Pickle in the parlour of our little village alehouse. (Johnson, pp. 23–24)

But there was a darker side even here. Charles's mother was more willing to have children than to commune with them once they were born. The maids would spend time with him, walking with him, telling him stories, listening to him, and entering his world. So would his father, as work permitted—but not so his mother. Charles was to grow up soul-hungry for a mother, and that never-to-be-filled void radically altered both his art and his life.

Dickens would also experience death at an early age. In today's society, most of our deaths occur from crime; from self-induced diseases like lung cancer; from automobile accidents; and from old-age afflictions. Charles's world was quite different: Crime-related deaths paled in significance when compared with deaths in childbirth or from childbirth complications (both mother and baby) and childhood diseases—all too often, they proved fatal; also, diseases such as smallpox, cholera, tuberculosis, diphtheria, measles, scarlet fever, whooping cough, and dysentery, as well as those resulting from antiquated medical care, abysmal sanitation, lack of fresh air, and poor hygiene, claimed thousands of victims.

Early on, young Charles perceived this fragility of life. Mary Weller often took him along with her when she went to lyings-in (in those days, babies were born at home) in her capacity as a midwife. Charles couldn't help but notice that babies died as often as they lived. "In one instance, a multiple birth had produced four or five dead infants, who were laid out, 'side by side, on a clean cloth on a chest of drawers,' which reminded him of pigs' feet as they are usually displayed at a neat tripe-shop" (Kaplan, p. 29). He would, of course, experience death again and again in his own family.

For a while, Charles attended nearby Giles School, where he felt he was on his way to becoming a gentleman. He studied penmanship, elocution, vocabulary, arithmetic, history, geography, and Latin—and he even won a prize for a recitation.

But in June 1822, without warning John Dickens was transferred back to London.

Adrift in London

To a child, moves are rather a lark—as long as things go well with Mother and Father, for they represent the home, not bricks, boards, steel, and glass. Consequently, Charles saw nothing ominous in another move.

But it didn't take long to unravel the secure blanket he had warmed his heart with in Rochester. He was permitted to stay one last summer in Kent, after which the ten-year-old boy was packed into a smelly coach—he was the only passenger—and sent to Cheapside in the rain. It was a most dreary ride. But arrival home was not much better. Everything was disorganized and confused, not only in the house itself but in that protective wall of fiscal solvency that parents erect around their children's sense of well-being. A bond was due, and John Dickens didn't have the money to pay it. The only way he could avoid disaster was to borrow more and cut back on expenses.

One of the first expenses to go was Charles's education: He was not permitted to return to school. Charles was desolate, for school had been opening up a new world for him. And it certainly didn't help when his parents somehow found enough money to send Fanny off to the Royal Academy of Music, but had none left for him.

All the while, there were continual knocks on the door as merchants and moneylenders demanded their money. And here and there, credit for the family's necessities began to be denied. John and Elizabeth appeared not to be unduly bothered by it all: He always felt "something would turn up" (à la Micawber), and she was so disorganized that one more problem wasn't enough for her to lose sleep over. But it was not so with Charles and Fanny—they were deeply humiliated by these fissures in their home walls. The very floor under their feet began to shake—and Charles, because he wasn't able to attend school, felt it most.

No one paid much attention to him, leaving him to putter around, do chores, watch over the younger children (there were now five in all), and run errands. He began to wander the streets of London—and these streets began to teach him a different kind of lesson. He saw "dirty men, filthy women, squalid children, fluttering shuttlecocks, noisy battledores, reeking pipes, bad fruit, more than doubtful oysters, attenuated cats, depressed dogs, anatomical fowls . . . and rotting cabbage. He began writing character sketches of those he observed" (Kaplan, pp. 35–36).

Neither John nor Elizabeth knew how to dig themselves out of their mess. Each had constructed a way of life. He tried to live as a gentleman, and she expected to live as she had as a child—a pampered member of the upper-middle class. In spite of their money woes, Elizabeth still perceived herself to be a woman of beauty and high culture, entitled to a comfortable life. Kaplan notes that neither was especially intelligent or hard-working; and they had neither strong religious convictions nor clear professional goals to help them establish long-range plans. Furthermore, they refused to recognize that self-denial was essential to survival.

When taxes came due, and they could not come up with what they owed, a summons was issued. And then another. At this juncture, George Lamert, an uncle, offered eleven-year-old Charles a job in his shoe-polish factory and warehouse; there, he could earn six shillings a week for the family coffers. His parents accepted the job for him.

Now Charles's dream of success and gentility seemed dead for sure. Two days after his twelfth birthday, the boy, stunned and in despair, reported for work. Some middle-class boys, less high-strung and sensitive than he, might have thrived in such an environment—but not Charles. Looking back a quarter of a century later, Dickens wondered how he could have been so cavalierly cast out of his home, and why "no one had compassion enough on me—a child of singular abilities, quick, eager, delicate, and soon hurt, bodily or mentally—to suggest that something might have been spared, as certainly it might have been, to place me at any common school. Our friends, I take it, were tired out. No one made any sign. My father and mother were quite satisfied. They could hardly have been more so, if I had been twenty years of age, distinguished at a grammar-school, and going to Cambridge" (Johnson, p. 31).

In truth, such child labor was the usual thing in nineteenth-century England. And the hours were anything but short: At the factory, the boys began work at 8 A.M. and didn't get to quit until twelve hours later, at 8 P.M.; they had only two breaks all day. The factory itself was a dilapidated old building on the Thames. It was filthy, and the smell of decay was omnipresent. There were rats everywhere: in the wainscoted rooms, in the rotten floors, in the crumbling stairway—and they could be heard continually as they swarmed throughout the building.

Charles had no idea of how desperate his parents' financial condition was, and what a relief it was to increase their cash flow, even by the small amount his work brought in. And on their part, they did not realize that their child was dying inside from the shame of having to work in a factory. It was not the job itself that humiliated him—"cover the pots of paste-blacking; first with a piece of oil paper, and then with a bit of blue paper; to tie them around with a string; and then to clip the paper close and neat, all round, until it looked as smart as a pot of ointment from an apothecary's shop" (Johnson, p. 32). On the finished product, he pasted a printed label. No, his shame wasn't because of the job; it was because his father had always encouraged him to be a gentleman.

Since the other boys had no pretensions of gentility, they felt instantly that Charles would not mesh—in fact, they called him "the young gentleman." In his autobiography, Dickens cried out,

No words can express the secret agony of my soul, as I sunk into this companionship; compared these every day associates with those of my happier childhood, and felt my early hopes of growing up to be a learned and distinguished man crushed in my breast. The deep remembrance of the sense I had of being utterly neglected and hopeless; of the shame I felt in my position; of the misery it was to my young heart to believe that, day by day, what I had learned, and thought, and delighted in . . . , was passing away from me, never to be brought back anymore; cannot be written. My whole nature was so penetrated with the grief and humiliation of such considerations, that even now, famous and caressed and happy, I often forget in my dreams that I have a dear wife and children; even that I am a man; and wander desolately back to that time of my life. (Johnson, pp. 32–33)

Eleven days after Charles began work at the blacking factory, his father was arrested for debt. He would spend the first three nights in what they called a "sponging house," trying to raise money and avoid imprisonment. Charles, his eyes filled with tears, spent the weekend shuttling messages back and forth for his weeping father. But it was all in vain: On Friday, February 20, John Dickens was taken to Marshalsea Prison. His last words to his son, before the gates closed behind him, were these: "The sun has set on me forever" (Johnson, p. 33).

At twelve years of age, the son had already exchanged roles with the father—never again could his father be to him what he had once been. For Charles, the two experiences of beginning work at the factory and having his father imprisoned for debt had taken the rest of his childhood away from him.

To this darkest period of his life, Charles would return later, in books such as the autobiographical *David Copperfield,* and try to exorcise the demons left within by these two experiences. But with Charles, nothing was ever lost: For he stored faces and mannerisms in his nearly photographic memory, to be held there until he had need of them—as sooner or later he almost always would. Even in debtor's prison, images were captured for the future: For instance, when his father sent him to the next floor to beg loan of a knife and fork, Charles saw "a very dirty lady in [the captain's] dirty room; and two wan girls, his daughters, with shock heads of hair. I thought I should not have liked to borrow Captain Porter's comb" (Johnson, p. 33). As Charles stood there, burning the scene into his mind, he instinctively knew that the two dirty little girls were the captain's "natural children" and the dirty lady was not his wife.

Though in prison, John Dickens retained his ornate, florid speech, but he was "dreadfully shaken. He became tremulously tragic; it may have been at this time that his son observed in his father that fluttering and frightened motion of the fingers about the lips that he later attributed to William Dorrit in the same misfortune" (Johnson, p. 34). And he had reason to be frightened. Either he remained here in prison—for he had no means to pay his debts—or he publicly admitted he could not handle money and availed himself of the last resort: the Insolvent Debtors Act. Of course, if he pursued the latter option, gone would be any chance he had of getting his job back: "Income, pension possibilities, all hopes, would vanish" (Johnson, p. 34). In desperation, John applied for early retirement on the basis of a chronic urinary problem.

Meanwhile, at home (if one could call it that) Charles's "distracted mother tried to keep things going, and the whimpering children fed, by pawning brooches and spoons [even the beloved books] and gradually stripping the rooms bare of furniture. At last there was nothing left in Gower Street but a few chairs, a kitchen table, and some beds; and the family camped out in the two parlours of the emptied house" (Johnson, p. 34).

Finally, it became clear that declaring insolvency was the only way out. The Dickenses would have to prove absolute destitution. One of the most humiliating days of Charles's life was having to report to the insolvency appraiser to see if what he wore would fall within the guidelines. He was deathly afraid they'd take his grandfather's silver watch ticking away in his pocket, but the official took one long look at the shabbily dressed boy and waved him out. It only took a moment, but that moment was seared into Dickens's consciousness for all time.

What came next, however, was even harder for the proud boy to accept. His mother and the four younger children left the now virtually empty Gower Street house and moved into Marshalsea Prison. True, it was crowded there—but it was also cheaper. And even more important, they were temporarily relieved from having to deal with all the irate, importuning creditors who laid siege to their home. In prison, the rest of the family could come and go at will—as long as they were back in before the outer prison doors were locked for the night.

Charles, however, was not included with the rest of the family; instead, a place was found for him to dwell, with a Mrs. Roylance, who unbeknownst to her, "unconsciously began to sit for Mrs. Pipchin in *Dombey* when she took me in" (Johnson, p. 35). Though his father paid for his lodging, all of Charles's food had to come out of the six shillings he earned at the factory.

So there he was: a smallish twelve-year-old boy adrift in one of the world's greatest cities. Years later, he wrote of these days that he had "no advice, no counsel, no encouragement, no consolation, no support, from anyone. . . . I know that, but for the mercy of God, I might easily have been, for any care that was taken of me, a little robber or a little vagabond" (Johnson, pp. 35–36). Undoubtedly, one of the reasons he remained so bitter at his mother was that here, during the darkest days of his life, his own mother had thrown him into the streets to sink or swim, drift into crime or stay above it, on his own. She didn't seem to care.

Not having to be accountable to anyone, Charles began roaming the streets like Harun al-Rashid of Baghdad, a thousand years earlier, and

O'Henry of New York, almost a hundred years later. He peered into every crevice, listened intently to every conversation, took stock of every characteristic, and assimilated every nuance of the great city.

On Sunday, his one day off, he would call for fourteen-year-old Fanny at the Academy of Music, and together they'd walk across Westminster Bridge en route to the prison, there to spend the day. On one of these evenings, he broke down completely. Listening to his broken sobs, his father emerged from his own troubles long enough to consider those of his son. As a result, he had Charles moved into a back attic close to Marshalsea; and from that point on, the boy was able to eat both breakfast (very early) and supper (very late) in the prison. Not even in his new home did Charles fail to observe the people around him: His new landlord was "a fat, lame old gentleman with a quiet old wife and an innocent grown-up son who was also lame" (Johnson, p. 37). The trio later became the Garlands in *The Old Curiosity Shop*.

Back in Marshalsea, John did not remain depressed for long. He assumed his usual lordly air, as if instead of being an inmate of the prison, he was actually the warden. The other debtors, most impressed, elected him chairman of the committee that did run their part of the prison. He did a superb job at it, treating with noblesse oblige "everyone from the turnkeys to the humblest inmate" (Johnson, p. 38). Dickens was good at this sort of thing. It was his own affairs that he couldn't manage. In spite of all the odds to the contrary, he blithely announced that things "were looking up." Strangely enough, he was right: His mother died, leaving him a legacy of £450. Thus John Dickens left prison a little over three months after he had entered it.

The Dickenses returned to Camden Town and took up temporary lodging. From there they moved to their shabbiest place yet. For some strange reason, during this period, Dickens was able to resume work at his old job at the navy office. Chesterton noted that Charles, by this time, "was no longer a normal boy, let alone a child. He called his wandering parent the Prodigal Father; and there was something of the same fantastic family inversion in the very existence of so watchful and critical a son. We are struck at once with an almost malicious maturity of satire; some of the best passages of prison life of the Pickwicks and Dorrits occur in private letters about his own early life" (*Britannica* VII, p. 331).

Week after week passed—and still Charles continued in his daily hell. To a child, today is all the time there is; both yesterday and tomorrow are irrelevant and meaningless. Thus to the sad boy, the boot-polish existence appeared to be eternal. But one day his father chanced to come into the factory at a time when Charles and coworker Bob Fagin were racing to see who could tie up the most pots in a short amount of time. Since they were the two fastest boys there, Lamert installed them next to one of the windows (he had moved the company to Covent Garden), so they could attract crowds.

Something about seeing his son in such a public role spoke to the father's pride, or perhaps even appealed to his sense of pity; at any rate, he wrote a zinger of a letter to Lamert. Now that he had a legacy from his mother, he could write such a caustic letter and not get hurt by it. Characteristically, he didn't confront Lamert personally but had his son hand-deliver the letter and thus receive the full, undiluted brunt of Lamert's anger. The upshot was that—to his great joy!—Charles was sent home.

But that was not the end of it, for his mother took an entirely different view of the matter. They needed the extra money, and who knew how long John's navy job would last? So, Elizabeth took it upon herself to go to Lamert and see if she could smooth over the quarrel and have Charles reinstated. She succeeded so well that she brought back an invitation for him to return to work the next day.

For once in his life, however, John Dickens bowed his back: Charles would not go back to that place—instead he would go to school. The battle raged, but Father held his ground. Many years later, Dickens drained some of the long-harbored venom he had for his mother by writing these words that even then were wracked with remembered anguish: "I do not write resentfully or angrily, for I know how all these things have worked to make me what I am: but I never afterwards forgot, I never shall forget, I never can forget, that my mother was warm for my being sent back [to the factory]" (Johnson, pp. 39–40).

So deeply was this burning memory buried that neither Dickens's wife nor his children ever heard of it until after he was dead. One thing is unquestionably true. So profound were the effects and so deep the rage, shame, humiliation, and raw pain experienced from the four to five months spent at the blacking factory and from the three months his family spent at Marshalsea that these intertwining dark valleys represent the dividing line between the child and the man. Charles was never able to think as a child or act as a child again. He determined that never again was anyone going to have such power over him. Most of his rage resulted from his parents' inability to handle their money wisely.

Up to this time, Charles had loved and respected them, in varying degrees. But now, he, first of all, no longer loved them as unreservedly as he once had; and second, he had lost most of his respect for them—and without respect, love rarely flourishes. Dickens, once he made up his mind on something, rarely looked back, and even more rarely did he change his mind. It was at this crucial watershed of his life that he first fully realized that if he was to become the success he dreamed of being, he could not expect much help from his father; and worse still, he could not expect any empathy from his mother, the one person from whom he ought to expect the most. And there was no question that if he did not direct his own destiny, and control his own earnings versus debt ratio, he would have no more future than his father did.

In essence, this twelve-year-old boy decided, on his own, that from this point forward, he was taking command of his own destiny.

Taking Charge

For a brief period, there was relative peace in Charles's life. His father enrolled him in Wellington House Academy, and there he studied for a couple of years. The school was probably neither better nor worse than most, but in terms of character contributions, Charles was able to add (in part or whole) "the vicious Squeers of *Nicholas Nickleby*, the fuming Creakle, the gentle Nell, and the absent-minded Dr. Strong of *David Copperfield*, the murderous M' Choakumchild of *Hard Times*, and the explosively repressed Bradley Headstone of *Our Mutual Friend*" (Kaplan, p. 45). The curriculum included Latin, composition, penmanship, geography, arithmetic, and French. Oh yes, and the value of money.

Meanwhile, at home, John and Elizabeth continued in the same jovial fiscal irresponsibility and mismanagement. In spite of two bequests, the Dickenses were continually being harassed by creditors, who attached just about everything John Dickens and his family owned. Always, it seemed they were on the run—keeping intact the family record of fleeing to another dwelling about once a year.

Charles was fifteen when his mother, always in need of money, arranged to have him drop out of school and become a law clerk at Ellis and Blackmore. Thus ended his life's formal schooling. Brief though it was, it was more than most children of that time received.

Charles was not impressed with the legal profession. About the only real benefit resulting from his rather boring job of registering wills, serving processes, and carrying documents back and forth, was that he became ever more knowledgeable about every building, byway, and forsaken corner of London. Not only did he study the different sections of the city—from Tower Hill to the Strand, from Hampton Court to Greenwich—but he also paid careful attention to the people themselves:

> He had seen the drunken revelers staggering home at early dawn and women bringing in baskets of fruit to Covent Garden Market, and long past midnight, watched the baked potato men and kidney-pie vendors closing their stalls in the neighborhood around Marsh Gate, and the Royal Coburg Theatre. "I thought I knew something of the town," said George Lear, remembering their days together at Ellis and Blackmore's, "but after a little talk with Dickens I found that I knew nothing. He knew it all from Bow to Brentford. . . . He could imitate, in a manner that I never saw equaled . . . the low population of the streets of London in all their varieties, whether mere loafers or sellers of fruit, vegetables, or anything else, and, besides these, all the leading actors and popular singers of the day, comic or patriotic." (Johnson, pp. 47–48)

While all this was happening, John Dickens permanently lost his navy office job; however, on the basis of twenty years of work and six children, he was granted a half-pension. But at forty-one, he couldn't live on that, so he set about learning shorthand; so enthusiastically did he throw himself into this new career that a year later he had become one of the elite Parliamentary Corps (transcribers) for the British Press. Charles was impressed enough with his father's efforts to shell out half a guinea for Gurney's shorthand textbook for himself.

Shorthand was only a tool for advancement, however. Drama, on the other hand, was life itself. Virtually every night found Charles in one of the cheap theater seats somewhere in London—from the major theaters at Covent Garden, Drury Lane, and Haymarket, to the "minor" theaters, and besides these, theaters of every possible kind.

Meanwhile, finding his salary frozen at Ellis and Blackmore, Charles moved on to Charles Molloy, a solicitor. But here, too, he was a young man in a hurry. Two months short of his seventeenth birthday, he concluded he could now hold his own with the best shorthand competitor, so he quit Molloy and joined a distant cousin on the Consistory Court of Doctors' Commons. Here he continued the apprenticeship in law that would one day make possible that judicial masterpiece, *Bleak House,* for the Doctors'

Commons included "the Admiralty Court; the Prerogative Office, where wills were registered and filed; the Prerogative Court, which dealt with Testamentary matters in the dioceses; the Court of Arches, which was the provincial court of the Archbishop of Canterbury; and the Consistory Court, which was the diocesan court of the Bishop of London" (Johnson, p. 49). Most of Charles's work was for the latter three.

His law apprenticeship represented only one part of Dickens's education. Another was made possible when he reached his eighteenth birthday: Finally he could secure a British Museum reader's ticket. During the next three to four years (his real college education), Charles immersed himself in Shakespeare, Addison, Goldsmith, Berges, Symonds, and other great thinkers, and he dug deeply into the history of England.

Along the way, he fell hopelessly in love with a bewitching little blonde beauty named Maria Beadnell. He was seventeen, hence still a bit naive about the world and the odds against his success. Given his low income and her higher station in life (her father was a moderately wealthy banker), he faced stiff odds. Unpropitiously, Dickens's father chose this period to declare insolvency again—not the best son-in-law recommendation to a hard-nosed banker.

Like most immature males of his age, Charles did not really know what he wanted—nay, needed—in a wife. Maria (two years older than he) was everything he should have avoided matrimonially. For one thing, she was too much like his mother: self-centered and frivolous. Though Dickens would obsessively pursue Maria for four years, clearly there never was much of a chance that her parents would sanction a marriage that socially appeared so undesirable.

Maria was flattered by Dickens's obvious surrender to her charms and his intensely eager courtship; he was also fun, intelligent, widely read, witty, a great conversationalist, and a hilarious mimic. All in all, he was a real asset in the parlor room. But she agreed with her parents about the unsuitability of the match.

At a party in 1833, Maria effectively squelched Charles's ardor by referring to him as a *boy*. "The word scorched my brain," Dickens recalled later (Kaplan, p. 53). Even so, Charles had benefited from his association with her, because in trying to win her, he had worked even harder at moving quickly up the career ladder.

All of his life—perhaps because he got so little from his mother—Charles yearned for love and appreciation. He had an insatiable need to daily be assured that he was worthy of being loved and appreciated. It was not enough that he had been told so yesterday: he had to be told again *today!*

Perhaps the theater could provide the daily adulation he craved. In March 1832, Charles made an appointment with George Bartley, manager of Covent Garden. In his request for an audition, Charles expressed belief in his gifts: "I have a strong perception of character and oddity and a natural power of reproducing in my own person what I observe in others" (Kaplan, p. 54). Fanny, now an instructor at the Royal Academy, agreed to accompany her brother with his repertoire of comic stories, songs, and skits.

But on the day of the audition, Dickens was laid up with a terrible cold— even his face was inflamed—so he was unable to audition. Writing Bartley, Charles thanked him and said he would resubmit his application for an audition the following season. In the meantime, he continued to produce and perform in dramatic productions, most often involving his family and friends. His father, now a portly journalist, always reveled in such things: performing as well as watching.

Dickens's final break with coquettish Maria Beadnell took place in May 1833. He would use her in his fiction, however, just as he would use almost everyone with whom he interacted. Dickens would portray Maria as a younger version of his mother: "the prototype of the flighty, self-indulgent coquette whose feelings never run deep enough to know and express real love" (Kaplan, p. 57). Kaplan notes that Dickens was attracted equally to two types of women: the Maria type "whose physical beauty and domineering manner attracted him erotically. Pain and pleasure, rejection and acceptance, were closely allied in his emotional life. Against that attraction, against women like Maria and his mother, he needed an antidote, a pure sister, an ideal wife" (Kaplan, p. 57).

Dickens had come a long way from the little boy who had reeled from the dual onslaughts of the blacking factory and the imprisonment of his father. But four years of unrequited love for Maria had taken their toll on him—and it did not assuage the bitter pain of rejection to know that, had his family status been higher and his career prospects brighter, she might indeed have become his wife. In fact, twenty-five years later she had the audacity to tell him so. At the very time when the entire Beadnell family began to blow frostily upon his suit, had they only known it, and waited a short time, the most famous author in the English-speaking world could have been part of their family.

But there is no question about one thing: Dickens had changed dramatically from the boy he had once been. Had his mother given him the love he so desperately needed, had Maria cared more for him than she did for status, then he might have been able to give a different kind of love than he did to his wife and parents. As it was, the crucible of pain and anguish resulting from a stingy dose of mother love; the insolvency, imprisonment, and continual humiliation attendant to his parents' inability to handle money; the terrible spirit-blighting of the blacking factory; and the rejection of the sincerest, purest, and most intense romantic love he would have in his lifetime, prepared him to write the kind of books that achieve immortality.

In November 1834, John Dickens was again arrested for nonpayment of a bill he owed a merchant; at the same time, he admitted to the family that because of nonpayment of the house rent, once again they were being evicted.

Charles concluded it was time to leave home for good.

"Boz"

The stenography expertise started it all. Two years after Charles began that career, he started another one. In 1831, John Henry Barrow, one of his uncles, asked Dickens if he'd be interested in contributing to his magazine, *Mirror of Parliament,* which printed transcripts of political debates much as the *Congressional Record* does today in the United States. Shortly after he began writing for the *Mirror,* Dickens also began to write for the *True Sun* (a liberal paper whose views he normally agreed with). But it was in *Mirror of Parliament* that he experienced the most rapid progress—not only in what he was paid but also in being offered editorial positions.

About this time, the chief secretary of the United Kingdom, Edward Stanley, had given a major speech dealing with conditions in Ireland. In fact, so long was the speech that the *Mirror* had eight reporters assigned to taking it down (with Dickens doing the beginning and the end of it). When the speech appeared in print, Stanley found errors everywhere—except in the first and last parts; he asked Barrow to send the reporter to him who so superbly recorded those parts of his speech. The praise given him by the secretary represented the high point of Dickens's life up to this time.

Parliamentary debate alternated between utter boredom and spine-tingling drama. The next debate after the Irish Coercion Bill became law had to do with the aftermath of Secretary Stanley's Bill for the Abolition of Slavery in the Colonies. During this memorable debate, Dickens recorded young Mr. Gladstone's maiden speech, as well as memorable speeches by Edward Bulwer-Lytton, Daniel O'Connell, and others.

Although Dickens faithfully and accurately recorded these debates, he was gradually becoming more and more disillusioned with the political process. So much of it was bombast and mere rhetoric—and so little of it improved the lot of the average citizen.

Along the way, Dickens, having a little extra time on his hands, began to write short fictional sketches based on people he had met and observed in and around London. One night he mailed to the *Mirror* a sketch satirizing a local politician. Not long after that, Dickens purchased the latest number of the magazine in a Strand bookstore. As he walked out, his heart was pounding: Would his piece have been considered good enough for inclusion? Turning a page, he saw his sketch there in all its glory.

So agitated was he that he walked on and on until he found a place of privacy in Westminster Hall. And there "for half an hour he paced the stone floor 'my eyes so dimmed with pride and joy that they could not bear the street, and were not fit to be seen'" (Johnson, p. 72).

The editor, Captain Holland, liked Dickens's sketch so much that in the next edition, he asked for the author to submit "more papers" (free, of course). Dickens did so, and five more were published during the following seven months. The earlier sketches carried no author identification, but starting with the August sketch, Dickens attached as his nom de plum "Boz." How did he come up with it? According to Johnson, it "had arisen out of Dickens' jesting nickname for his seven-year-old brother Augustus . . . whose nasal mispronunciation of Moses as 'Boses' was facetiously adapted and shortened to 'Bose' by the time Dickens borrowed it for his own pseudonym: 'Boz was a very familiar household word to me, long before I was an author'" (Johnson, p. 73).

The very same month that "Boz" was born, Dickens had begun work for the *Morning Chronicle*. The editor, John Black, was a scholarly but determined philosophical radical. Within only a couple of years—no small thanks to the popularity of Dickens's writing—he was able to increase the daily paper's circulation 600 percent—to 66,000, making it second in circulation only to the famed *London Times*. From this time on, Dickens's life became more interesting, as Black had him cover the most significant stories of the day, some taking him as far away as Scotland. By now, Dickens had seen and recorded so much that government officials no longer impressed him—so he felt free to inject humor into stories dealing with them. As a case in point: "At another public dinner, when the Earl of Lincoln floundered through a few halting words and resumed his seat in confusion, Dickens reported:

'Lord Lincoln broke down, and sat down'" (Johnson, p. 75).

By late 1834, the identity of the increasingly popular "Boz" sketches was no longer secret, and Dickens was pointed out as a young man who would go far. But even his £275 salary proved insufficient to cover his and his family's expenses. It didn't help much that his "prodigal father" had done it again: His recent employers had let him go, and now he owed so much that arrest was imminent. Characteristically, the good man fled, leaving his wife and children to face whatever music was performed by the creditors. Poor Charles decided that, like it or not, he'd have to step in and salvage something out of the mess. At considerable sacrifice and tightening of his own budget, he worked out a solution: For the rest of his life, he would pay his parents' bills.

On January 31, 1835, a far-reaching event occurred, but not for the reason one might expect: The proprietors of the *Morning Chronicle* launched another paper, which they called the *Evening Chronicle*. George Hogarth, music critic for the morning paper, was chosen as the editor. One of Hogarth's first decisions was to ask Dickens if he would be willing to submit sketches similar to his "Street Sketches." Dickens agreed. Hogarth had been a writer to the Signet (an elite law practitioner) in Scotland and was a friend of Robert Burns and Sir Walter Scott—in fact, his sister had married James Ballantyne, one of Scott's closest business associates. Hogarth had had his eye on Dickens for some time, so now, with Dickens agreeing to submit twenty sketches during the next seven months, the friendship deepened. Hogarth invited Charles to visit his family at home—not an entirely altruistic gesture, as he had ten children, among whom were three attractive daughters: Catherine (the oldest at nineteen), Mary (at fifteen), and Georgina (at seven). Johnson describes Catherine as being "a pretty girl with a rosy complexion, heavy-lidded blue eyes, and a slightly retroussé nose" (Johnson, p. 78). Kaplan describes the eldest in more detail: "With heavy-lidded eyes and turned-up nose, Catherine had a becoming tendency to carry her shortness into full-figured plumpness. Though not quick of wit or foot, she was warm, engaging, eager to please and to be pleased, and clearly on the marriageable side of adolescence. Unlike Maria [Beadnell], she was not flirtatious or fickle" (Kaplan, pp. 66–67).

Dickens now had more clearly defined marital goals and expectations than had been true when he courted Maria: First of all, he wanted a woman who would consider him to be the center of her life; second, recognizing that he was marrying more than a wife, he wanted her family to provide an intimacy and stability that was lacking in his, and, if possible, to also be one in which the world of the mind and the arts was central. Furthermore, having had enough rejection to last a lifetime, he wanted someone who would not be likely to refuse him. All these elements, he found in Catherine (Kate) and the Hogarth family.

Dickens was not at all concerned that Catherine would be incapable of keeping up with him in terms of imaginative thought. He was twenty-three now, and rising rapidly professionally; it was time for him to marry. "With a strong sense of having been deprived of a familial hearth, he used the Hogarths' as the threshold of his own. Marriage to an amiable, conventional, sweet-tempered, and domestic woman, who would cooperate with his desire to be master of his own home, to be in control of his life and work, to have compliant, contained, and unthreatening sexual relations, to have children with whom to express his own familial needs, was strongly attractive" (Kaplan, pp. 67–68). Charles proposed, and Catherine accepted. As it turned out, in Catherine and the Hogarths, Dickens got everything he wanted. The package was responsible for the explosion of creativity ahead; unfortunately, it was also responsible for a different kind of explosion at the end.

Dickens was sincere in his commitment to Catherine: In return for having a bedrock of faithfulness at home (on which he would build a life, a career, a legacy, and an estate), he would be faithful to her. Catherine was correct in her assumption that she—her heart, soul, mind, and dreams—was not as central to him as he was to her. But she married him anyway. Dickens leased some rooms next door to the Hogarths and alleviated space constraints with the two families by adding to his household his brother Fred and her sister Mary. Charles and Catherine were married at St. Luke's Church, Chelsea, on April 2, 1836. Dickens's close friend Thomas Beard served as best man.

The ceremony, wedding breakfast, and one-week honeymoon to Gravesend Road in the little village of Chalk (near Chatham) were alike simple. Dickens chose Chalk because it was in Kent, the site of the only Shangri-La he had ever known. His bride was very different from "the tiny and teasing charmer with enchanting ringlets" Maria Beadnell, for Catherine was "a full-bosomed lass with long, dark hair and a sleepy voluptuousness" (Johnson, p. 89) that perhaps helped account for the fact that she was pregnant before the week was over and would be pregnant—seemingly almost continuously—throughout their marriage. Ten children would survive.

Mary, Catherine's younger sister, idolized her brilliant brother-in-law. She, it turns out, might very well have been the perfect wife for him instead of her more prosaic sister. To Dickens, Mary possessed the ingredients missing in

Catherine: intelligence, the ability to understand and empathize with his creative genius, numerous virtues, unquestioned loyalty, and budding beauty. "She became," Dickens said, "the grace and life of our home; so perfect a creature . . . never breathed" (Johnson, p. 94). She was the ideal girl-wife.

Meanwhile, exciting things were happening to Dickens. All his life, he would juggle a thousand-and-one projects, manuscripts, involvements, responsibilities, and deadlines. At this time, his newspaper and magazine reporting kept him forever on the go—politically, nothing happened that he wasn't a part of, in one way or another.

However, for three years, the "Boz" sketches had been building an audience for him. Late in 1835, Dickens and Beard put together a collection of the best of the sketches and landed George Cruikshank as the artist. That was no mean coup, because Burne Jones, the Rossettis, Sickert, Whistler, and others prophesied that Cruikshank would someday be known as the greatest English artist of the nineteenth century.

Although Cruikshank would illustrate only five Dickens books (twenty-four would be illustrated with pictures) out of the nearly 900 he would illustrate over his long and impressive career, both men profited by their brief (1835–1841) association. Today, Cruikshank's fame rests more on his Dickens illustrations than on any others he did. Sadly, their egos eventually wrecked their relationship. Before "Boz," Cruikshank, the idol of millions, was so famous that he was paid not to caricature kings. Though Dickens knew what his characters ought to look like, Cruikshank had his own ideas. A terrific struggle for control ensued. Dickens won, and his star continued to rise; Cruikshank lost, and his star began to sink.

Sketches by Boz: Illustrative of Every-Day Life and Every-Day People was published by John Macrone on February 7, 1836, Dickens's twenty-fourth birthday. In the two volumes were sixteen Cruikshank illustrations. Macrone paid Dickens £150 for all rights; he received no royalties. Copies were sent to VIPs such as Lord (Edward John) Stanley, members of Parliament such as Thomas Noon Talfourd, and many editors. While reviews were favorable, the best were Hogarth's and John Forster's (who would become one of Dickens's closest friends). Snatches from these reviews include:

> "He can sympathize with the underpaid milliners' and staymakers' [corsets'] apprentices, and pity the scantily clad ballad singer with the wailing child whose only reward from the passing crowd is 'a brutal laugh at her weak voice.' Such sights, he says, 'will make your heart

ache—always supposing,' he bitterly adds, 'that you are neither a philosopher nor a political economist.' Well-bred ladies and gentlemen might do something more generous and useful than recoil from the sixteen-year-old streetwalker whose features are already branded with depravity 'as legibly as if a red-hot iron had seared them' and whose later career 'in crime will be as rapid as the flight of a pestilence . . . in its baneful influence and wide-spreading infection.'" (Johnson, p. 84)

Such commentary was prophetic, for Dickens would go on to become perhaps the most powerful social critic of the age.

By August, *Sketches* had gone into its second printing, and during 1837, it went through two more. Even more important, the success of the book attracted the attention of two gentlemen whose fortunes would intertwine with those of Dickens: the publishers Edward Chapman and William Hall. They came to him with a proposal: Would he like to collaborate on a project with well-known illustrator Robert Seymour? Seymour, born out of wedlock, was a slightly unbalanced but extremely talented artist, best known for his slashing caricatures of the hunting set—those wealthy Englishmen who had nothing better to do with their time than ride around slaughtering birds and animals.

The project Chapman and Hall had in mind was a series of plates illustrating the adventures and misadventures of the mythical Nimrod Club (a group of amateur sportsmen); the central figure would be "Mr. Nathaniel Winkle." Seymour's sketches would be the meat of the work; Dickens's text would provide pleasing commentary. Several other writers had already turned down the commission before it was offered to Dickens.

But Dickens was no pushover. In fact, he brashly seized control of the project, suggesting that, instead of his writing Seymour-induced commentary, Seymour should illustrate Dickens's prose. And central to his prose would be Pickwick instead of Winkle. The result was more than a bit funny, for Dickens thought Seymour was illustrating his prose and Seymour thought Dickens was describing his art. But there was one serendipity: Seymour did depict Pickwick so vividly that he gave him immortality—"made him a reality"—and Dickens's text had given him precious little to go on. As the tug-of-war continued, Seymour, already furious about a non-Dickens-related situation where he had been publicly ridiculed, went over the edge and took his life. Hablôt Knight Browne (known as "Phiz") took over and thereby rose to fame with Dickens on the astounding success of *The Pickwick Papers*. For the rest of Dickens's life, Seymour's widow continued to demand additional recognition and money; he, however, adamantly refused to help her.

Pickwick began life inauspiciously, as Chapman and Hall only gambled 400 copies in the first printing. Subsequent sales continued in the doldrums, and Dickens filled the waiting time with projects such as writing the lyrics for John Braham's "The Village Coquettes." As late as the fourth issue (almost all of Dickens's books were first issued serially), *Pickwick's* sales were still sluggish—but in that fourth installment, Dickens, in a stroke of genius, introduced Sam Weller. By July, interest in *Pickwick* began to build—then it became a torrent, with 40,000 copies sold of every issue. Reviewers now raved about it, and it became the rage of the season.

Johnson notes that "readers in every class of society became Mr. Pickwick's devoted admirers and followed his adventures from month to month with roars of loving laughter" (Johnson, p. 110). Dickens had created a new literary form, a fairy tale that was simultaneously humorous, heroic, and realistic. Pickwick was "a beaming fairy godfather to almost all the world, forever rescuing maidens and bestowing them on their true loves, succoring the oppressed, showering even the cheats and petty tricksters with his kindness. His very existence and personality represent[ed] a kind of magic; if not that of an ugly ducking turned into a swan, [than that of] a very foolish goose transformed into an angel in gaiters" (Johnson, p. 110).

By the time the last green-covered number of *Pickwick* had hit the stands, "they had become a mania. Nothing like it had ever happened before. . . . It is doubtful if any other single work of letters has ever aroused such wild and widespread enthusiasm. *Barely past the age of twenty-five, Charles Dickens had become world-famous, beaten upon by a fierce limelight which never left him for the remainder of his life*" (Johnson, pp. 110–11, emphasis added).

Olympus

The world was at Dickens's door. The son of an insolvent ne'er-do-well was now the toast of London—and soon, the world! It was a heady feeling for such a young man.

About this time, Charles's marriage to Catherine began to unravel. Had they started out marriage alone—just the two of them—they might have bonded. But with two strangers in the house—Fred and Mary—family members or not, a tension was created that might otherwise not have been there.

While Charles courted Catherine, Mary had become like a sister to him. Apparently always happy, and so helpful she rapidly proved to be indispensable, Mary soon became the joy of the household. Usually, in a marriage, a husband and wife need to work through their differences, but, as Johnson points out, a monkey wrench had been thrown into the Dickenses' marital machinery: "When the third member [Fred had left earlier] of the family is a beautiful and adoring young girl who admires her sister's husband beyond measure, it is easy for him to believe that any flaws in the serenity of his home are no fault of his, and it is easy for him, too, without quite realizing that he is doing so, to exalt the younger sister at the expense of the other" (Johnson, p. 97). Exacerbating the situation even more was Catherine's amazing fecundity: The bloating we associate with pregnancy often puts a strain on a marriage, for the wife loses the figure she had before, especially as she nears full-term. If she no sooner delivers one than she becomes pregnant with the next—and a beautiful sister is there to shine in her stead, trouble is likely to result. To his credit, Dickens remained faithful to his wife—that did not turn out to be the problem.

It was a Saturday evening, May 7, 1837, and Dickens's new comedy, *Is She His Wife?* was being performed in the St. James Theatre. Mary never looked lovelier than she did that night as she leaned "her sweet face" over the edge of the box. The play had to do with two intertwining young marriages that weren't going well—certainly reflected by lines such as, "How little did I think when I married you six months [ago] that I should be exposed to so much wretchedness," and "If you are perpetually yawning and complaining of ennui a few months after marriage, what am I to suppose you'll become in a few years?" (Kaplan, p. 93). The marital bickering at home must have come to mind as Mary watched the drama unfold—though not, perhaps, as bad as to warrant Dickens's contention many years later that "Mary . . . understood . . . in the first months of our marriage 'that the marriage was as miserable a one as ever was'" (Kaplan, p. 93).

After the performance was over, they returned home. Soon after midnight, Mary became violently ill. Doctors were called in, and the Hogarths came from next door. Mrs. Hogarth was almost hysterical with fear. The doctors concluded that Mary had a weakened heart and had experienced a stroke. Charles, Catherine, and Mrs. Hogarth stayed with her all night. Sunday afternoon, Charles administered some brandy to Mary as he held her in his arms. Before sinking into a gentle sleep, she whispered to him, and her very last words were of him, he later wrote. She died at three that afternoon. "The light and life of our happy circle . . . passed quietly away to an immortality of happiness and joy," wrote Dickens. Catherine was more succinct: "'I never saw her look so lovely and the next [day] she was dead'" (Kaplan, p. 93).

Mary's death almost destroyed Dickens, for she had indeed been the light of their lives. *Pickwick* came to an absolute halt—in fact, Dickens could not write a word. It was the only time in his life that he was incapable of meeting a deadline. Three months pregnant, Catherine miscarried.

As for Dickens, he never completely recovered from his sister-in-law's death. To him, it was just another form of rejection: the first had been his mother's maternal rejection; and the second, Maria Beadnell's romantic rejection. "Idealized as the female who genuinely loved him and whom he could trust, Mary had been elevated into the perfect sister: She had sympathized 'with all my thoughts and feelings more than anyone I knew ever did or will'" (Kaplan, p. 94). Significantly, Kaplan notes that the "faultless Mary had been a better mother, a better sister, an alternative Catherine, a completion of Catherine, adding insight, sympathy, and intelligent understanding" (Kaplan, p. 94).

The terrible downside for the stricken Catherine, had she fully realized it, was that her sister would prove to be a far greater rival in death than she ever could have been had she lived and gotten older, for she was frozen at maximum beauty and perfection—for all time. Now nothing Catherine could ever say, do, or be could possibly compare with the image Dickens retained in his heart and mind of this lost sister.

It is a measure of his grief that Dickens worded Mary's tombstone as he did:

MARY SCOTT HOGARTH
Died 7th May 1837
Young, Beautiful, and Good
God in His Mercy
Numbered Her with His Angels
at the Early Age of
Seventeen

For years, Dickens hoped that when he died, he might be buried with her.

The memory of Mary would powerfully affect the books Dickens wrote. A good example of this is *Oliver Twist,* which Dickens began five months before Mary died, the same month his first son, Charles Culliford Boz Dickens, was born. *Oliver* (published in 1839) was, in fact, the first book in which he came up with a plot before he wrote the story. Most of it was written in the year and a half after Mary's death and is extremely autobiographical. It was a voyage in which Dickens traced his own pattern of early and continual rejection; in his fiction, this rejection is usually portrayed in the person of an orphan (Oliver, Pip, Little Nell, David Copperfield, Esther Summerson) or a child who has lost one parent (Nicholas Nickleby, Florence Dombey, Amy Dorrit). Oliver's mother, unlike his own, dies in childbirth, "young, beautiful, and good"—to Dickens, the perfect expression of unqualified love (Kaplan, p. 96).

About a year after Mary's death, Dickens introduced the beautiful seventeen-year-old Rose Maylie into *Oliver Twist*. She represents Dickens's lost angelic sister: too good, too sweet, too pure, to be long for this earth. Yet, in the end, Dickens cannot let Rose go and lets her live instead. As Johnson puts it: "When he was drawing near the end of *Oliver Twist*, he found himself unable to carry out his original intention of having Rose Maylie die. He could not bear to describe the fair young creature breathing her last amid the blossoms of May" (Johnson, p. 127).

But *Oliver Twist* is far more than a memorial to Mary—and a far cry from rollicking *Pickwick*—for in it, for the first time, Dickens moves in his biggest reform guns, aimed primarily at England's antiquated and inhumane Poor Law and at the heartbreaking conditions endured by those forced to exist in London's appalling slums. The book does have comedy, but it is a comedy that bites. Johnson points out that it took courage for Dickens to abandon a sure thing in *Pickwick* and follow up that lighthearted book with such a somber, bitter, and serious portrayal of the darker side of urban life. In *Oliver Twist*, Dickens hit his stride, for readers loathed Fagin and Sikes with all the intensity that they had loved Pickwick and Weller.

G. K. Chesterton notes that Oliver is "not only the first of [Dickens's] nightmare novels, but also the first of his social tracts." And that, furthermore, Dickens was already showing his mastery of unforgettable lines, such as "in that intolerable repetition throbbing in the murderer's ears: 'will wash out mud-stains, bloodstains'" (*Britannica* VII, p. 332). *Oliver Twist* was the first book for which Dickens used his own name. From then on, his real name and "Boz" were used interchangeably.

For some time, Dickens had been gathering his forces for an attack on Yorkshire schools. Though they claimed to be offering a quality education at bargain prices, in reality they were "notorious for negligence, cruelty, and pedagogical incompetence" (Johnson, p. 137). Other "schools" were actually dead-end hellholes for illegitimate and other unwanted children. Dickens gathered information for this book by traveling under an assumed name and doing on-the-spot research. Titled *Nicholas Nickleby*, the book sold 50,000 copies on the first day it appeared in print.

Interestingly enough, *Nicholas Nickleby* was a synthesis of *Pickwick* and *Oliver:* According to Chesterton, "*Pickwick* has a prevailing tint of gaiety and *Oliver Twist* of gravity, not to say grimness; but with *Nicholas Nickleby* (1839) we have the new method, which is like a pattern of light and dark stripes" (*Britannica* VII, p. 333). "Vain, ineffectual, and verbally comic" Mrs. Nickleby, by the way, is patterned after Dickens's own mother (Kaplan, p. 119).

Chesterton also notes that, though the book has major weaknesses in it, it is saved by the marvelous characters with whom Dickens peoples it—for example, Vincent Crummles, Miss Snevellici and her "incomparable" father, and Mr. Mantalini.

Off and on during his life, Dickens turned back to the format of a magazine, in order to broaden his financial net even more. (He had signed a lucrative agreement with Chapman and Hall, having learned much about his marketability since his naive beginning, when he'd take whatever was offered.) In 1840, Dickens started a new weekly magazine titled *Master Humphrey's Clock.* Although sales started briskly, they dropped off precipitously when readers discovered there was no ongoing serialized story. In order to recapture them, in June of that year, Dickens began a new novel, *The Old Curiosity Shop.* It was a sentimental age, and Dickens took full advantage of that fact with this particular book. Little Nell became one of his most famous characters, both in England and in the United States. As the story progressed and Dickens neared her probable death, readers became more and more apprehensive, begging him to not let her die. And he, remembering again the death of Mary, found it difficult to continue the story.

The Old Curiosity Shop has much to say about nineteenth-century greed and speculation—especially on the stock exchange. Thanks to the tear-inducing addition of this story, *Master Humphrey's Clock* came back to life again. As it neared its end, up to 100,000 copies of each issue were being sold.

Kaplan notes that Little Nell's improvident grandfather is yet another in a long line of failed fathers in Dickens's fictional gallery. As a result, the orphaned Little Nell is forced to father her grandfather and to become both mother and father to herself, mirroring Dickens's own childhood.

Meanwhile, much had been happening in Dickens's personal life. His closest circle of companions now included writers such as John Forster, Thomas Carlyle, Lord Edward Bulwer-Lytton, William Makepeace Thackeray, Wilkie Collins, Leigh Hunt, and Harrison Ainsworth; artists such as John Leech, George Cruikshank, Daniel Maclise, Hablôt Knight Browne; actors such as William Charles Macready and Walter Savage Landor; journalists such as Thomas Beard, William Henry Wills, and Mark Lemon; and politicians such as Thomas Noon Talfourd and Charles and Edward Landseer.

At home, life was generally serene. By the mid-1830s, his parents had only their youngest, Augustus, at home. As for his mother, according to Kaplan, by the early 1840s, "she balanced matriarchal stoutness with some affectations of youthfulness, particularly 'the juvenility of her dress' and her semi-comic confusions of speech. Her son described her wardrobe as 'the attempt of a middle-aged mutton to dress itself lamb fashion'"(Kaplan, pp. 118–21). Although he frequently had his folks over for dinner on Sundays and holidays, Dickens kept his emotional distance from his mother.

As for his father—much as he loved him, Dickens was often enraged by his finding ever new ways of trading on his son's fame in order to secure extra transfusions of money. Occasionally, father and son would endure stormy sessions, scenes in which "his father played the role of the prodigal son. Dickens accurately described his father as 'an optimist—he was like a cork—if he was pushed under water in one place, he always bobbed up to time cheerfully in another, and felt none the worse for the dip'" (Kaplan, p. 103). Finally, reaching the end of the proverbial rope, Dickens decided to exile the "governor" and his lady to an attractive little house in the beautiful but quiet countryside of Alphington, near Exeter. Dickens gave them an allowance that should have covered all their needs. For them, though, who were by now a bit afraid of their famous son, it seemed like rejection, and the remote location like an exile. "For him, it was self-protection with a touch of revenge" (Kaplan, p. 105).

As Dickens's own family grew, he periodically moved them to larger quarters. In March 1838, his first daughter was born—he named her Mary (Mamie) Hogarth Dickens; eighteen months later, Catherine (Katey) Macready Dickens followed her. Catherine usually had tough pregnancies and was often ill during and after them. Her sister's death had deeply affected her, and for a long time afterward, she was in a deep depression. After her daughter Mary's birth in 1838, she was "alarmingly ill" for some time. But the children kept coming: Walter Savage Landor Dickens came next, in 1841.

Every summer, Dickens would take his family to the seaside (to towns like Brighton and Broadstairs), to the country, or across the Channel to the Continent. These vacations were not just for the immediate family; they often included extended family and friends as well.

Back in London, Dickens was involved in many clubs: the Trio Club, the Cerberus Club, the Shakespeare Club, the Parthenon Club, the Garrick, the Athenaeum Club, and so on. Founded in 1824, the Athenaeum Club invited only the elite to its membership: the leading scholars, men of letters, artists, scientists, and statesmen. In June 1838, Dickens was inducted into the club, along with such men as Macready and Charles Darwin. Thackeray had to wait until he was forty to be invited in, Browning until he was fifty-six.

In June 1841, Dickens and Catherine traveled to her native Edinburgh, where he was treated like a monarch at a public banquet. He was introduced as "perhaps the most popular author now alive" (Kaplan, p. 113). After dinner, Catherine led 200 ladies to the gallery to hear the toasts and speeches. It was so crowded that people were turned away. "As Dickens came through the door, and entered the hall, the orchestra struck up, to 'tumultuous applause' and 'shouts of delight,' the popular music-hall song, 'Charley Is My Darling'" (Kaplan, p. 116). The rest was a royal progress.

In his negotiations with publishers, illustrators, and other members of the literary field, Dickens developed into a shrewd and almost brutal bargainer. According to Johnson, Dickens never surrendered even the smallest point to his adversary. In his obsession to win, he was relentless. This iron-gloved determination would make him the wealthiest writer in the British Empire— but it would also make him unnecessary enemies and bring him great sorrow.

Twisting the Sword

The Old Curiosity Shop was followed by *Barnaby Rudge* in 1841. This book was Dickens's first attempt at historic fiction. It's also unique in that it is considered to be the first detective novel. Closest perhaps to Scott's *The Heart of Midlothian*, it deals with the historic Gordon riots and the burning of the Newgate Prison by an infuriated mob. Dickens treated his protagonist Lord George Gordon, whom he drew from English history, better than many felt he deserved. Describing the writing process, Johnson notes that "as his imagination plunged into the surging tumults of the riots themselves, Dickens' emotions boiled up in a strange turmoil. Fear and horror of the ferocities of mob violence struggled with his fierce sympathy for the wrongs of the oppressed rising like fiends to avenge themselves in destruction. He obviously shared with the rioters an orgiastic joy in the flaming demolition of Newgate amid clamor and smoke. He shuddered and at the same time he exulted in this overflow of authority" (Johnson, p. 183).

Coloring the picture, undoubtedly, was the image of Marshalsea Prison staining his childhood. The actual riots of 1780 were the historical basis for the story, but his contemporary readers saw in it current events—such as the deep industrial depression, the Chartist movement for universal suffrage and equal representation in Parliament, the riots of Welsh miners in 1839, the empty cotton mills and their jobless workers walking the streets, and the entire north of England on a great strike that was dispersed only by troops firing point-blank into the crowds.

But in this book, Dickens was doing more than merely entertaining. He had just read "with anger and horror" the report of the Children's Employment Commission, which gave accounts of dark mining tunnels reeking with poisoned air, in which seven-year-old children were chained to heavy carts and brutally forced to drag them; of "girls clad only in ragged trousers working in the dark, often up to their knees in water and carrying heavy loads of coal up steep ladders a distance exceeding the height of St. Paul's Cathedral; of dreadful accidents constantly occurring; of deformed and stunted boys toiling fourteen hours a day, fed on offal, struck with bars, burned by showers of sparks from red-hot irons, pulled by the ears until the blood ran down" (Johnson, pp. 184–85).

Barnaby Rudge is grimly prophetic, and in it Dickens tells England's power brokers that unless they voluntarily make reforms now, it will later prove too late as they are swept away in a tidal wave of blood à la French Revolution.

Now occurred an event of far-reaching significance: In 1842, Dickens decided to visit the United States. Catherine went with him. He was thirty years old and as famous in America as he was in England. However, the United States caused Dickens to grind his teeth in frustration because of that nation's refusal to honor international copyright laws and pay him royalties. Beginning in 1834, pirated editions of Dickens's books had begun to be sold in immense quantities in America. He was hopeful, however, that the United States would prove to be a utopia, a community of friends, a model of Christian rhetoric put into everyday practice. In short, everything England was not. Dickens and Washington Irving had been corresponding for some time, so they both looked forward to meeting each other. Dickens hoped Irving would guide him to the nation's most congenial thought-leaders.

All America turned out to honor Dickens, and he was besieged by fans wherever he went. He quickly discovered that Americans, unlike the English, neither understood nor respected personal space. In fact, Dickens felt more like a captured lion than an honored guest. The newspapers sensationalized his every move. "Soon he felt so beset, waylaid, hustled, sat upon, beaten about, trampled down, mashed, bruised, and pounded by crowds" that he felt everything was out of control (Kaplan, p. 127).

While Dickens was sitting for a portrait in Boston, "ladies pressed into the studio to stare at him until Dickens bolted for the door, only to be mobbed there and forced to retreat and lock himself within. When hunger obliged him to emerge for lunch they were still besieging the doorway, and surged about him instantly again, clinging to him while they furtively snipped bits of fur from his [buffalo] coat as souvenirs and filling the passage with a soprano clamor of adulation" (Johnson, pp. 202–203).

Letters poured in to such an extent that within three days, Dickens had to hire a secretary, George W. Putnam. Even while eating, Dickens would sign autographs. Though he never turned down a request for an autograph, "he drew the line at gratifying the numerous young ladies who wanted locks of his hair" (Johnson, p. 203).

Dickens initially planned to write a positive book on Americans and the United States. He was most impressed by the Perkins Institute for the Blind—especially that the children were not forced to wear ugly uniforms. And he was "deeply moved by the loving success with which Dr. Samuel Gridley Howe and his helpers taught blind, deaf, and dumb children how to communicate with their fellows and develop into intelligent and cheerful human beings. He was strongly impressed by the use of kindness and of occupational therapy in the State Hospital of the Insane" (Johnson, p. 205). Especially did he note the thoughtful touch of potted plants in the windows. Longfellow and Charles Sumner personally conducted him on a walking tour of Boston, visiting the waterfront, Paul Revere's house, and the Bunker Hill monument; and before parting, Longfellow invited Dickens to break-fast with him at the Craigie House the following Friday.

Determined to see more of the United States than just Boston and New York, Dickens set out on a hectic trip through rural America. He began by taking the train to Philadelphia, Baltimore, and Washington. Along the way, he was appalled at American hygiene—or, rather, the lack of it—especially the widespread habit of spitting saliva and tobacco juice into spittoons, but not caring too much where the nasty stuff landed. The sides of trains tended to be speckled with spit much as if a monstrous flock of birds had paid their compliments. And whenever the train stopped, heads popped in, "bawling out, 'Is Mr. Dickens here?'" (Johnson, p. 209). During Dickens's New York stay, Irving came down the Hudson and hauled him up to his Tarrytown estate, Sunnyside; William Cullen Bryant was there, too.

Used to fresh air and milder winters, Dickens had a tough time dealing with overheated interiors, for Americans evidently didn't believe in opening windows during the winter. Franklin stoves were everywhere, heating rooms to a most uncomfortable level for the British couple.

In Baltimore, Dickens had a long chat with Edgar Allen Poe. In Washington—which the British had burned almost to the ground thirty years earlier—Dickens met Henry Clay, former president John Quincy Adams, and Daniel Webster; he also had a private audience with President Tyler. To Dickens's disgust, even in the White House, visitors picked their teeth and constantly spat tobacco juice on the carpet.

In the South, Dickens felt as if he were in prison because of the treatment of slaves. He could hardly wait to get away from that region. Going west, Dickens and his wife took the train twelve miles outside of Baltimore, where the track ended. From there, the couple traveled by stagecoach or steamboat. At Harrisburg, they boarded a canal boat, headed to Pittsburgh, then took a steamboat to Cincinnati; from there, they went to St. Louis, Missouri; to Cairo, Illinois; then north to Toronto, Montreal, and Quebec. At the end of 1842, they stood by Niagara Falls, of which Dickens rhapsodized: "This great place . . . the most wonderful and beautiful in the world" (Kaplan, pp. 136–39). On one leg of the journey, poor Catherine was showered all night with flying tobacco spittle from a well-dressed man sitting next to them. Dickens decided they could not handle another experience like that, so at Columbus, he hired a carriage just for them. This form of transportation proved to be not much of an improvement. The roads were rough, and the Dickenses were constantly being tossed into the roof of the carriage, slammed against the sides, and ignominiously heaved onto the floor. As for Catherine, she was unmoved by most things—except the bedbugs—and even Niagara Falls, to her, was only so much water.

Then it was back to New York, via stagecoach, steamboat, and railroad. From there, they boarded a ship for home, having been gone half a year. "On shipboard, [Dickens] played perpetually on an accordion that he had bought in March and on which every night he had played 'Home Sweet Home' as they had traveled through America" (Kaplan, p. 142).

On the way home, Dickens realized that he had not won the victory over the greedy interests that were against copyright reciprocity with England. In fact, it would not be until twenty-one years after his death that the United States, kicking and screaming, finally joined the larger world community and began paying authors royalties.

Just before leaving Montreal, Dickens had written Forster: "As the time draws nearer, we get FEVERED with anxiety for home. . . . Kiss our darlings for us. We shall soon meet, please God, and be happier and merrier than ever we were, in all our lives. . . . Oh home—home—home—home—home—home—HOME!!!!!!!!!!" (Johnson, p. 235).

Once home, they were engulfed by the children, and Dickens spent hour after hour playing games with them, rocking the younger ones on his knee—in a rocker he brought over from the United States—and singing silly songs to them.

A parting gift in America had been Timber Doodle, a little white Havana spaniel. When he reached home, Dickens renamed the dog "Snittle Timbery" and gave each of the children a loony name, too: Charley became "Flaster Floby," a corruption of "Master Toby"; to her infinite amusement, quiet little Mamie he dubbed "Mild Glo'ster"; fiery-tempered Katey became "Katey Lucifer Box"; and baby Walter, because of high cheekbones, was christened "Young Skull."

Then Dickens went to work on *American Notes*, his account of, and reactions to, the United States and Americans. Most of the book was Boz-like: a series of impressions. Dickens minced no words about the things he didn't like—especially slavery and the copyright pirating. Friends were concerned about the reception such a book might receive—as well they should have been, knowing Dickens's tendency, once opposed on something, to bull-headedly do it anyway. They were afraid that Americans, still being new to the family of nations, would be thin-skinned about his criticism.

Longfellow arrived for a visit and had a wonderful time with everyone—especially the children (who loved him) and the Dickenses' "pet" raven, Grip, "a talkative and rambunctious bird . . . who alarmed the children and lady visitors by pecking at their ankles" (Johnson, p. 175). The bird served as a model for his namesake in *Barnaby Rudge*. When Grip died, Dickens wrote some of his friends about the last touching moments: "A bird fancier was first called in to administer a powerful dose of castor oil. The next morning, much better, Grip 'so far recovered his spirits as to be able to bite the groom severely.' But he had a relapse, in which he talked to himself incoherently. 'On the clock striking twelve he appeared slightly agitated, but he soon recovered, walked twice or thrice along the coach-house, stopped to bark, staggered, exclaimed Halloa old girl (his favorite expression), and died'" (Johnson, p. 240).

While the Dickenses had been gone, Catherine's youngest sister, Georgina (now fifteen), had spent a lot of time with the children. So much did they rave about her and clamor for her that she was invited to become part of the family, just as Mary had been—and she quickly proved herself indispensable to all.

At the same time that he was wrestling with *American Notes,* Dickens was trying to bring his next novel to life. He had a terrible time finding just the right name for the book and its hero: "Sweezleden," "Sweezlewag," "Chuzzletoe," "Chuzzleboy," "Chubblewig," and "Chuzzlewig" were considered and discarded en route to "Martin Chuzzlewit."

As originally conceived, there was a theme of selfishness and the vices that are spawned by it—and, in spite of the book's many turns and twists, that theme remained a constant. Johnson feels that "the vast gallery of multiple perspectives on selfishness is dazzling—young Martin, thoughtless and self-indulgent; his domineering grandfather; an entire tribe of snapping, snarling, greedy Chuzzlewits, salivating for the family fortune; hypocritical and pontifical Pecksniff; the brassily glittering swindler Tigg Montague; the fraudulent land speculator Zephaniah Scadder; . . . the menacing frontier bully, Hannibal Chollop," and so on, make this an incredibly riveting saga (Johnson, pp. 242–43). But the two characters that really run away with the story are "the snuff-stained and feisty Sairey Gamp and the bland and unctuous Pecksniff" (Johnson, p. 244).

Despite the concerns, *American Notes* sold like wildfire on both sides of the Atlantic. In New York, 50,000 sold in two days, and in Philadelphia, 3,000 sold in thirty minutes. Reviews were mixed: Many thought Dickens's picture of America was too harsh.

In contrast to *American Notes,* the British sales for *Chuzzlewit* were sluggish. Since *American Notes* was selling well in the United States, Dickens decided to hurl Chuzzlewit across the water to America and leave him there to see if he could thereby help to sell more books in England.

It certainly appeared that Dickens was biting the hand that had fed and entertained him in that new nation. *American Notes* was bad enough, but to stir in the ugly greed of *Chuzzlewit* was twisting the sword in the wound with a vengeance. In the United States, the book aroused a veritable firestorm of fury. Even though Dickens had expected to stir the Americans up, he had not expected such virulence or outrage. All he had done in *Chuzzlewit* was to portray American culture as "essentially materialistic, immoral, greedy, hypo-critical, and debased" (Kaplan, p. 157). Surely they couldn't be upset over a little thing like that!

But there was another part of the fallout from the sluggish British sales of

Chuzzlewit that was rather sad. In an unwise moment, William Hall groused about the low sales and muttered something about maybe reducing Dickens's royalties proportionally. Always thin-skinned about money, Dickens, upon hearing Hall's remark, began to think of changing publishers, which he did after *A Christmas Carol* was out. Though Chapman and Hall had always been fair to Dickens, and the three men had become dear friends, Dickens would not return to them for sixteen years. To Dickens, friendship came second in any business deal. There was more than a little of Chuzzlewit in his own dealings.

During all these years, Dickens reveled in his family. He loved to celebrate, and his joie du vivre was most infectious. For instance, he put on a big celebration each year, tying in his oldest son's birthday, Christmas, and Twelfth Night with a professionally done extravaganza of "charades, magic shows, pantomimes, and elaborate amateur theatricals." Since Dickens loved to dance, dancing was very much a part of the agenda as well. And no Twelfth Night celebration was complete without Dickens putting on a magic show, with Forster playing the straight man.

Itchy Feet

It is indeed ironic how sometimes the work we put into the "smaller" projects during life turns out, in retrospect, to be the most significant. After *Chuzzlewit's* sales refused to rise, Dickens needed money, and he cast about for a quick way to earn some. *A Christmas Carol* was the result. The irony comes from the inescapable fact that if every other story he wrote should fall out of favor, *Carol* would survive.

Strangely enough, at the time Dickens wrote *Carol,* the old Christmas traditions were on the decline and actually in danger of being lost. Dickens has been credited with almost single-handedly bringing them back (Hearn, p. 1).

The year 1843 was a strange time in Dickens's life to have written such a Christmas book: The American tour had not been a success; even less so—at least in terms of readership and critical response—had been the slashing anti-American attacks in *American Notes* and *Chuzzlewit;* to say nothing of the undeniable fact that the latter represented the first significant ebb in book success for Dickens in quite a few years. For the first time, he had to face the possibility that he might have peaked and that the rest of his life would be all downhill. His family expenses were high—and now Catherine was pregnant again, with their fifth child.

But Dickens's life and career had one constant: He never ceased caring. Especially did he care about the poor, the downtrodden, the disadvantaged, and the children. On October 5, 1843, he had shared the Athenaeum stage with the man who would go on to become one of the British Empire's greatest prime ministers: Benjamin Disraeli. The subject of the day was the poor and the need for education. The audience's applause was so enthusiastic and supportive that Dickens couldn't get the subject out of his head. Wasn't there some way he could do more?

During a three-day visit to Manchester, Dickens's mind kept returning to want and ignorance. One evening, en route to an appointment, the story concept of *A Christmas Carol* was born. Hearn notes that "on his return home, this inspiration so possessed him that over the book's writing he 'wept and laughed and wept again, and excited himself in a most extraordinary manner in the composition; and thinking whereof he walked about the back streets of London, fifteen and twenty miles many a night, when all sober folks had gone to bed" (Hearn, pp. 8–9).

For the root of the story, Dickens relied on his own earlier narrative, "The Goblins Who Stole a Sexton," wherein Gabriel Grub, a mean-spirited gravedigger, is taken by goblins to their den, and there they reveal to him, through panoramic imagery, how Christmas really ought to be observed. Dickens borrows, too, from his Christmas writings in *Pickwick Papers* and *Sketches by Boz.*

But *Carol* moves on from there into uncharted waters. The theme Dickens articulates, and which he never lets the reader forget, is that Christmas "is a time of all others, when Want is keenly felt, and Abundance rejoices" (Hearn, p. 13). In this story, finally Dickens had a vehicle for an appeal to the people of England on behalf of the poor man's child.

Having chosen the theme, Dickens created Scrooge next; in his boyhood state—even to the books he loves—Scrooge is Dickens himself. The pathos of Tiny Tim, Dickens drew from those in his own family who had died as children or teenagers. The Ghost of Christmas Present clearly articulates the plight of children in mines and schools like the ones in Yorkshire that Dickens had studied firsthand.

As momentum increased, Dickens dropped everything else in his obsession to stay with his characters—for his characters were every bit as real to him as any friends or loved ones in actual life. For a month and a half, he lived, slept, and dreamed the story, delivering it to Chapman and Hall in mid-November. Apparently, neither partner was optimistic about potential sales for the book, so they proposed a cheap edition. In the end, Dickens decided to take all the risks himself, including the cost of the illustrations (color and black-and-white). Compounding the earnings problem, Dickens insisted that the lovely little book (russet binding, stamped in gold, colored endpapers, gilt edges, and the title page printed in two colors) be sold for only five shillings so it would be available to everyone.

A question some might ask is this: What effect did finishing the book have on Dickens himself? According to Hearn, "At the completion of the manuscript, the Christmas fervor still burned within him, and when the holidays did arrive, he celebrated them with an exuberance that his friends (including Forster, Thackeray, and Carlyle) had not witnessed before. 'Such dinings, such dancing, such conjurings, such blind-man's bluffings, such theatre-goings, such kissings-out-of-old-years and kissings-in-of-new-ones, never took place in these parts before,' he wrote Felton" (Hearn, p. 14).

He did not have long to wait for the reading public's verdict: The sales were tremendous—on Christmas Day alone, 6,000 copies were sold. Reviewers were kind as well. Edgar Johnson summed up the book's philosophy in these words: "Dickens insists that no way of life is sound or rewarding that leaves out men's need of loving and being loved. *A Christmas Carol* is a serio-comic parable of social redemption, and Scrooge's conversion is the conversion for which Dickens hopes among mankind" (Johnson, p. 257).

Because of the double whammy of a luxurious book for a pauper's price, Dickens's original profits were almost nil—and he badly needed the money. He was devastated. His entire earnings for his first Christmas season added up to only £726.

Having established the Christmas genre, during the next few years, Dickens followed *Carol* up with *The Chimes* (1844), *The Cricket on the Hearth* (1845), *The Battle of Life* (1846), and *The Haunted Man* (1848). The second and third titles did well; the last two considerably less so. But Dickens was never again to write a Christmas story anywhere near as powerful as the story of Scrooge and Marley.

Eventually, the combination of the trip to America, changing publishers (to Bradbury and Evans), and undulating sales, plus the itch to try something new, all combined to give Dickens the worst case of wanderlust yet. Then, too, pirates really moved in on *Carol*. Dickens took them to court, but lost money, as most of the culprits merely folded and ran away with their earnings. As a result, Dickens tended, in the future, to just bite his lip and let it go when other unscrupulous publishers stole from him.

Frances Jeffrey Dickens was born in January 1844. By now, Dickens was complaining about the regularity with which new mouths and appetites arrived at his door, and he blamed poor Catherine: "I hope my missus won't do so never more" (Kaplan, p. 158). He never seemed to feel it necessary to acknowledge that he might have had a tad to do with this increase himself.

So, they decided to go to Italy. The caravan consisted of (according to Dickens):

1. The inimitable Boz;
2. The other half ditto;
3. The sister of ditto ditto;
4. Four babies, ranging from two years and a half to seven and a half;
5. Three women servants, commanded by Anne of Broadstairs. [The baby (the fifth child) was added to the party at the last minute.] (Johnson, p. 266)

On July 2, 1844, the entourage set out, complete with Snittle Timberry, barking excitedly. Dickens was in high spirits, like a boy out of school, and delighted to be leaving society. He was "aweary of it, despise[d] it, hate[d] it, and reject[ed] it" (Johnson, p. 269). Other than that, society was fine.

Once across the Channel, Dickens secured a behemoth of a coach for £45. Soon it, with the Dickens's entourage inside, was on the way to Paris. Describing it, he wrote Forster: "Let me see—it is about the size of your library; with night-lamps and day-lamps and pockets and imperials and leathern cellars, and the most extraordinary contrivances" (Johnson, p. 269). Their passage caused all the excitement a 100-cannon windjammer would generate in a quiet harbor. The eleventh day out saw them on a grimy vessel crossing the Rhone.

Arriving at Marseilles, their carriage was hoisted to the deck of the *Marie Antoinette* "amid a Vesuvius of Profanity" as it bumped against everything around it (Johnson, p. 271). In time, they disembarked at Genoa and were dismayed at the filth and stench of the streets. Since the streets were narrow and the carriage wasn't, it was forever scraping or jamming. At last they came to their long-anticipated palazzo: "an archway with a rusty and sagging gate opening on a rank, dull, weedy courtyard attached to a building that looked, Dickens reflected, like a pink jail. His heart sank. This 'lonely, rusty, stagnant old staggerer of a domain' was the Villa de Bella Vista!" (Johnson, p. 272).

The next day, they discovered that if you didn't shut the lattice blinds—

which took away your view of the Mediterranean—"the sun would drive you mad; and after sunset the windows had to be shut, 'or the mosquitoes would tempt you to suicide'" (Johnson, p. 273). They survived Villa de Bella Vista (Villa of the Beautiful View) until late September, when they moved to the Palazzo Peschiere (Palace of Fishponds), which had seven fountains, each with fish. Inside was the grand sala, fifty feet high, and two bedrooms larger than any in Windsor Castle. It was a veritable wonderland for the children to play in.

In this idyllic setting, Dickens continued to cast around for a story line. Suddenly, it seemed as if all the church bells of Genoa were clanging at once. Thus was born his second Christmas book, *The Chimes*, a story pleading for charity and justice for the dead-end poor.

Upon completing the manuscript in November, Dickens decided to deliver it personally to his publisher in England. Leaving his family behind, he traveled to Parma, Bologna—and then Venice, which dazzled him as had few wonders during his lifetime: "The wildest visions of the Arabian Nights are nothing to the Piazza of Saint Mark and the first impression of the inside of the church. The gorgeous and wonderful reality of Venice is beyond the fancy of the wildest dreamer" (Johnson, p. 281).

From there he went to Milan, across the Alps by moonlight, through Paris, and across the Channel to England again. After seeing that his manuscript was in good hands, Dickens took a ship to Genoa and was back with his family in time for Christmas.

Dickens was not to find writing as easy in Italy as in noisy, turbulent London. They decided to travel some more. Upon seeing Rome, Dickens initially was not impressed—but then he saw the Coliseum, and from that time on, he began to fall under the spell of the Eternal City. Later, the Dickenses moved on to Naples; they climbed Vesuvius and looked down into the boiling cauldron. By mid-June, they were back in England again, complete with a manuscript titled "Pictures from Italy."

Alfred D'Orsay Tennyson Dickens was born on October 28, 1845; both the Count D'Orsay and Tennyson were there, godfathering the christening celebration.

But Dickens's dry spell continued—in fact, it was one of the longest of his career. During these years, he and his family traveled some more throughout Europe, but the muse seemed gone from him. Finally, in Lausanne, on June 28, 1846, Dickens was able to write Forster and tell him the good news: BEGAN DOMBEY! He began it with a determination to use it as a vehicle for getting back his audience. Because of that goal, he didn't take chances: He incorporated into the plot only what had heretofore worked for him. Chesterton puts it this way: "[I]t has very much the character of the winding up of an old business, like the winding up of the Dombey firm at the end of it. It is as comic as the earlier books were comic, and no praise can be higher; it is as conventional as the earlier plots were conventional, and never really pretended to be anything else" (*Britannica* VII, p. 334).

Dombey represents the first time Dickens chose the protagonist from the aristocracy rather than from the people. It bridges back to *Chuzzlewit* in that the story reveals that the power of love is ultimately greater than the power of money. Dombey is a powerful symbol of the money-centered society Dickens knew and the belief that money can buy everything.

Captain Cuttle and Mr. Toots are among the great portraits in the book. Florence Dombey, like Ruth Pinch in *Chuzzlewit,* is another reincarnation of the loving spirit of the long-since-departed Mary Hogarth; and the pathos of Paul Dombey's life also is in the same almost-too-good-for-this-world vein. Yet at the same time, much of Paul Dombey is autobiographical and hence bridges to David Copperfield.

Dombey was written in different parts of Europe—key sections were completed in Genoa, Switzerland, and Paris, where Dickens met his idol, Victor Hugo, as well as Alexandre Dumás and Eugène Sue. Along the way, Catherine gave birth to their seventh child, Sydney Smith Haldimand Dickens.

Dombey roared along, becoming ever more successful, as the various installments hit the streets. Never again was Dickens to have money problems. But an ominous note surfaced during the last part of the book: the disintegration of Dombey's marital relationship was being mirrored by his own. As Catherine got older and experienced one pregnancy after another, her appearance suffered, and she began to appear, in Dickens's own words, "tremendously fat" (Kaplan, p. 237). Just as bad, husband and wife communicated poorly—so much so that Dickens began to despair as he looked down through the years and saw nothing ahead but loneliness of mind. He certainly could have found plenty of beautiful women who would have eased that loneliness for him, but unlike many of his closest friends who did have affairs, his moral code was more rigid than theirs.

The House on Gad's Hill

Dombey reminded Dickens of himself as he once was, and the birth of the dreams that had taken him to his unparalleled eminence. With his next book, Dickens would go even deeper, to see if he could find not only his earlier self but perhaps the answers to the questions that were gnawing on his happiness. So it was that in 1849—at the age of thirty-seven—Dickens began one of his greatest books: *David Copperfield*. Chesterton describes the book as a "romantic biography"—which is not bad, "for romance is a very real part of life and perhaps the most real part of youth. Dickens had turned the telescope round or was looking through the other end of it; looking perhaps into a mirror, looking in any case out of a new window. It was life as he saw it, which was somewhat fantastically; but it was his own life as he knew it, and even as he had lived it. In other words, it is fanciful but it is not fictitious; because not merely invented in the manner of fiction" (*Britannica* VII, p. 334). Chesterton goes on to point out that the way Dickens breathed life into stock characters, as he did in *Pickwick* and *Nickleby*, was quite different from what he did in *David Copperfield*. The way Dickens perceived the key characters in the book was the way any youth would have seen them, for young people have a different perspective on life than do adults: "There are men like Steerforth and girls like Dora; they are not as boys see them; but boys do see them so. This passionate autobiography, though it stiffens into greater conventionality at the real period of passion, is really, in the dismally battered phrase, a human document" (*Britannica* VII, p. 334). Chesterton then wraps up his analysis of *Copperfield* with a most provocative addendum: Evidently, *Copperfield* must have accomplished what Dickens hoped it would, for never again would Dickens replow that old ground. The book represents the dividing line between what Dickens was and what he was becoming.

One of Dickens's key motivations to look backward almost certainly was the untimely death of Fanny, his closest sibling, of tuberculosis in 1848. She had been dying for two years. By May 1848, she was coughing incessantly and could only achieve temporary relief by taking morphine. During her last weeks, Dickens haunted her bedside—as did their father. Dickens wrote Catherine that "no words . . . can express the terrible aspect of suffering and suffocation—the appalling noise in her throat—and the agonizing looks around" (Johnson, pp. 338–39). Fanny died on September 2. She was thirty-eight years old.

In 1849, Henry Fielding Dickens (child number eight) was born on January 15. That same year, Dickens completed a little book—today virtually unknown—that is significant to Christians: *The Life of Our Lord*. In it, he tried to portray to his children, and to other readers, what Christ's love and ministry were all about.

Dickens did not return to *David Copperfield* until after Fanny died. The protagonist of the story was originally called "Thomas Mag"—then "David Mag"—and finally "David Copperfield." Dickens had perfect pitch when it came to deciding on names for his characters. He was startled when Forster pointed out that the initials were his own, reversed. The Micawbers are, of course, immortal—especially Mr. Micawber (so much of his father is poured into his "cork-ship"). Dora is Maria Beadnell, only sweet and gentle. In no other book he ever wrote did he dare to reveal so much of himself, and of this he always remained conscious: "'Like many fond parents,' he said, 'I have a favourite child. And his name is David Copperfield'" (Johnson, p. 355).

When Dickens finished the book on October 21, 1850, he wrote Forster, expressing his ambivalence—his oscillation between joy and pain. He concluded the letter with: "Oh, my dear Forster, if I were to say half of what Copperfield makes me think to-night, how strangely, even to you, I should be turned inside out! I seem to be sending some part of myself into the shadowy world" (Johnson, p. 355).

In March 1850, Dickens began another major project, publishing a weekly family magazine he called *Household Words.* The magazine would go on to feature some of the nation's most famous authors and to become one of the most widely read in England. Over the next nine years, its weekly sales would average 40,000 copies! A number of Dickens's books would be serialized in it, including his two-volume work: *A Child's History of England.*

Dickens's ninth child, Dora Annie Dickens, was born in August 1850.

The next year, 1851, was rough: Dora was gravely ill, Catherine was ill both physically and psychologically, and Dickens's father was dying. On March 31, after enduring a horribly painful and bloody prostate operation—without the benefit of chloroform—John Dickens died. Dickens was there in time, but his father was past recognizing him. Johnson poignantly observes, "As he looked at his father's dead face, where were the grandiloquence, the improvident borrowings, the irresponsibility, the disappearances to escape the bailiff? He could remember only the hard work, the irrepressible gusto, the old companionship of walks to Gad's Hill, the loving pride in a small boy's singing, the tenderness that throughout many a night had nursed a sick child" (Johnson, p. 376).

Barely two weeks later, after having appeared to recover, little Dora suddenly died in convulsions.

On May 16, Dickens and his theatrical company put on Bulwer-Lytton's play *We're Not as Bad as We Seem*—it had been postponed because of Dora's death—for Queen Victoria and Prince Albert.

In March 1852, Dickens's tenth and last child, and one of his favorites, was born: Edward Bulwer Lytton Dickens (nicknamed Plorn: mercifully abbreviated from Plornishghenter).

On the heels of *Copperfield* came *Bleak House,* as powerful an attack on the British legal system and bureaucratic gobbledygook as has ever been written. Its beginning is famous for the greatest extended metaphor of weather—in this case, fog—ever featured in a work of literature. The fog's counterpart is the Court of Chancery, an institution Dickens knew well from his court-reporting days. The case, based on an actual one, has to do with a legal duel over the considerable assets left to two children (in the book, the case is known as Jarndyce and Jarndyce). Though it takes them three generations, the lawyers manage to milk every last penny out of the "inheritance." The novel is all-encompassing and the attack is multidimensional.

Mrs. Jellyby is one of Dickens's most wondrous creations: the wealthy do-gooder who drives everyone bonkers with her fund-raising for overseas charity needs; yet she couldn't see a real one at home if it ran over her. Esther Summerson is a synthesis of Mary and Georgina. All three sisters ended up giving their lives to Dickens. Georgina, too, was captivated by his genius and, in time, became the keeper of the sacred flame, proving herself absolutely indispensable to him.

One of the really tough aspects about the writing of *Bleak House* has to do with Dickens's use of two first-person narrators: one male, one female. Wilkie Collins declared that it "contains . . . some of the finest passages he has ever written . . . brought out with such pathos, delicacy, and truth, as no living writer has ever rivaled, or even approached" (Kaplan, p. 288).

Johnson's capsulization of the book is itself a work of art (keeping in mind that when Dickens was writing the last pages of *Bleak House* in August 1853, there was a siege of stormy weather at the same time):

> There is a poetic fitness about this nocturnal violence that marked the close of *Bleak House,* for it is a dark and tempestuous book. The fog choking its opening scene, the rain swirling over Ghost's Walk at Chesney Wold amid the dripping funeral urns on the balustrade, the black and verminous ruins of Tom-all-Alone's crashing at intervals with a cloud of dust, the besmeared archway and iron-barred gate that lead to the rat-infested graveyard, insinuate their oppressive gloom even amid the genial sunlit scenes. A turbulent and furious hostility to vested evils storms savagely through its pages. (Johnson, pp. 396–97)

So exhausted was Dickens after finishing *Bleak House* that he, Wilkie Collins, and Augustus Egg left on a two-month holiday in Switzerland and Italy. Upon his return, Dickens put on the first public readings from his works: He read for three hours from *A Christmas Carol,* in front of 2,000 spellbound listeners, followed by another three hours from *The Cricket on the Hearth.* He did *Carol* again on November 29, specifically for 2,500 poorer workers.

After *Bleak House* came another powerful social novel, *Hard Times* (1854), Dickens's first story of outright social protest. Earlier books had contained sections of social criticism, but this book was a frontal attack. Dedicated to another critic of contemporary society, Thomas Carlyle, it is based on personal observations of life in Manchester, one of England's great manufacturing centers. Unfortunately for Dickens's credibility, however, the bad guys are such monsters that they seem stereotypical rather than real. As to the conditions that caused Dickens to write the book, here is what Johnson has to say:

Chimneys smutted the sky and killed grass and trees, chemical waste fouled the streams, bleak miles of tenements spread like a cancerous blight over the countryside. Row upon row of flimsy houses, three quarters of them with no privies, crammed thousands of human beings into damp rooms and cellars. Heaps of ordure and garbage outside drained into ditches which provided the only water people had to drink. The owners of the factories fought by every evasion against obedience to the Ten Hours Bill, cynically defied sanitary regulations in unventilated workrooms, and recklessly ignored the law requiring that dangerous machinery be fenced in. (Johnson, p. 405)

Dickens was irate enough about the conditions themselves, but what made him livid was the deliberate ignoring of the landmark legislation that was supposed to protect workers from the industrialists who considered human life to be less important than making money. Dickens wrote *Hard Times,* a 100,000-word book, in one nonstop whirlwind of energy and concern, finishing on July 17, 1854.

In the book are revealed other fissures in Dickens's house, such as female dependency (reminding one of that experienced by Mamie, Katey, Georgina, and Mary). John Dickens can be seen in the redemption of Thomas Gradgrind, as well as in the negative picture of Mr. Bounderby; Mrs. Sparsit is another revealing picture of his mother. Catherine can be seen in Stephen Blackpool's wife: her "incompetence, clumsiness, withdrawal from responsibility, and unsuitability" (Kaplan, p. 310).

On his forty-third birthday, with snow four to six feet high on either side of the road, Dickens once again cast eyes on his childhood dream house, the Georgian mansion that crowned Gad's Hill. And it was for sale! Dickens had never owned property before—wouldn't it be fitting, his life being the fairy tale it was, if he could own it? He set about to buy it and then spent additional money bringing it up to his exacting specifications.

It is said that there are two tragedies in life: when one's dreams fail to come true, and when one's dreams do come true. Both chose this moment to coalesce.

Here was Dickens—after a lifetime of living in houses, large and small, comfortable and cramped, at last having the opportunity to not only live in but also buy his childhood dream home. What more could one ask life to give him? Two days after his birthday, he chanced to look down at some mail, looked away, then swiveled back: There was something familiar about that handwriting! He had seen it before—long, long ago. Yes, no question about it. It was a letter from Maria Beadnell. "Three or four and twenty years vanished like a dream, and I opened [her letter] with the touch of my young friend David Copperfield when he was in love" (Kaplan, p. 323).

As Johnson tells the story, Dickens opened the letter with a shaking hand. He did remember hearing that Maria had not married until the ripe old age of thirty-five, and to a man who was neither distinguished nor wealthy. Now the shoe was on the other foot, and she was writing to him, asking if they could reestablish the old friendship. She was still married and had two little girls; but that hadn't kept her from trying to rekindle a long-dead flame with one of the most famous men in the world. He must see her! Over the next few weeks, they corresponded, before finally setting up a time and place to meet—privately. Dickens did not really intend to reignite a romance with her—that was long since dead. But it would be delightful to perhaps flirt a little. Considering the dying of his love for Catherine, who knew what might happen . . . if the chemistry was still there. In one of his letters, Dickens told Maria that she had been the catalyst for all he had become.

Finally, the day came for their meeting. He had expected her to look older—after all, she was forty-five:

Nevertheless, for all her warning, he was surprised to find her so undeniably fat. But it was not the physical change that was shattering. The gay little laugh had turned into a silly giggle. The delightful little voice, running on in such enchanting nonsense, had become a muddleheaded and disjointed volubility. The pretty pettish flirtatious little ways, the arch glances and tones of voice that suggested a secret understanding, were merely ridiculous affectations in a middle-aged woman. What had happened to the fascination that had captivated him? Or, still worse, was it possible that Maria had always been this absurd and brainless chatterer, that her angelic charm had been only the radiant hallucination of youth? (Johnson, p. 419)

Even more terrifying, this stout monster, "tossing her head with a caricature of her girlish manner, throwing him the most distressing imitations of the old glances, behaved as if this private meeting involved them in some intimate agreement. But 'this grotesque revival' of what had 'once been prettily natural to her,' was now like an attempt to resuscitate an old play 'when the stage was dusty, when the scenery was faded, when the youthful actors were dead, when the orchestra was empty, when the lights were out'" (Johnson, p. 419).

These were the words to describe the impact on him of seeing Maria Beadnell again after all those years—only the name he gave her was Flora Finching, and the book (his next) was *Little Dorrit*.

It would have been better for Dickens—certainly, better for his family—had he learned his lesson from this attempt to rewrite the past. But it was not to be: The letter from Maria Beadnell is the Pandora's box of the rest of his life. The letter set in motion feelings that perhaps might otherwise have died still-born, or at least have been unacted upon. And he had had to follow through, meet with her family, listen to her twaddle as she chirped by his side, even catch her cold, and then find ways to avoid being cruel as she attempted to resume the old relationship.

Originally, Dickens had intended to call the new story *Nobody's Fault*—but moments before publication, he switched to *Little Dorrit*. The experience with Maria had profoundly shaken him, unsettled his equilibrium, forced him to reexamine his rosiest contentions.

Today a book dealing with imprisonment for debt would appear far-fetched, but to readers of Dickens's day it was no joke. Of course the book was much more than a mere re-creation of Marshalsea: It was an attack on a vast, disembodied bureaucracy that apparently had to be accountable to no one. Dickens also stirred in rack-renting of the poor, extortion, and sinister collusion at the top.

Dickens wrote part of *Little Dorrit* in England (in the middle of bull-

headed government resistance to reform and corrupt and inefficient admin-
istration of the bloody Crimean War) and part of it in Paris (in the middle
of a speculative frenzy). The result was a brooding darkness. And by the time
he got to the revisionist portrayal of Maria Winter née Beadnell as portrayed
by Flora Finching, he was beginning to chortle at the drollness of the whole
thing. Of course he couldn't laugh too much, for Maria didn't look much
different now from Catherine. Both were fat, and both, he felt, were difficult
to communicate with. Little Dorrit herself is yet another re-creation of Mary
and Georgina Hogarth.

For the first time since *Pickwick,* Dickens returned to a debtor's prison as
a setting. For years, rather than see it, he would detour. Even though John
Dickens is not William Dorrit, there was enough of his father in the
character to disturb him. And Mrs. Clennam is perhaps the most horrible
and frightening example of bad mothering in all his fiction.

On May 11, 1857, *Little Dorrit* was completed.

Best of Times, Worst of Times

We now come to a play coauthored by Wilkie Collins and Dickens that
really became a play within a play. Collins's name was on it and the title was
The Frozen Deep, a melodrama based on the ill-fated polar expedition of Sir
John Franklin—all the members had died of starvation or exposure. Dickens
played the romantic lead, as Richard Wardour, a rejected suitor of Clara
Burnham. Presaging *A Tale of Two Cities,* Wardour rescues his successful rival,
Frank Aldersley, and then dies with Clara's tears raining down on his face. Its
first performance was on January 6, 1857.

Meanwhile, Gad's Hill was finally his! The Dickenses began moving in.
One of their first guests was Hans Christian Andersen, who stayed a bit too
long: five weeks (four weeks and four days longer than Benjamin Franklin's
proverbial three-day limit).

Queen Victoria, Prince Albert, and the king of the Belgians were given a
private performance of *The Frozen Deep.* But then, in late August, the play
was to be performed in an immense auditorium; so large, in fact, that only
an experienced actress could "make her actions seen and her voice heard";
consequently, substitutes had to be found for Katey and Mamie, as well as
for most of the other female members of the cast. The suggestion was made
that Dickens consider "the well-known actress Mrs. Ternan and her two
daughters, Maria Ternan and Ellen Lawless Ternan" (Johnson, p. 445).
Dickens (as stage manager) assigned the part of Nurse Esther to Mrs. Ternan,

the part of Clara Burnham (the heroine) to Maria (the more experienced of the two sisters), and Lucy Crawford (a minor role) to Ellen. At the performance, Dickens surpassed himself, leaving the audience in tears. The second night—with 3,000 in the audience—was just as powerful.

The play coincided with a period of deep despair for Dickens—despair because he felt he was living in a loveless marriage and could not get out. Divorce, in Victorian England, was unthinkable. Furthermore, he and his writings represented part of the rock upon which societal morality was based. To all other appearances, Dickens seemed to have a perfect everything—especially his home life. Dickens wrote Forster, saying, "Poor Catherine and I are not made for each other, and there is no help for it. It is not only that she makes me uneasy and unhappy, but that I make her so too—and much more so" (Johnson, p. 448). Then Dickens went on to admit that this state of affairs had existed ever since the days when Mary, his first child, was born.

Forster countered that there were no perfect marriages—most people had problems of some kind. But Dickens would not accept such a solution in his case: "Too late to say, 'put the curb on, and don't rush at hills,' Dickens responded wearily, '—the wrong man to say it to. I have now no relief but in action. I am incapable of rest. I am quite confident I should rust, break, and die, if I spared myself. Much better to die, doing'" (Johnson, p. 449).

This is a sad part of Dickens's story. Suffice it to say that shortly after moving to the dream mansion on Gad's Hill, the Dickenses separated. The marriage was not dissolved; she and the children had visitation rights, and Georgina stayed on as de facto mother and person in charge of day-to-day activities and events (for she was extremely capable where Catherine was not).

Unquestionably, however, this separation had a major impact on the children, resulting in Katey's escaping into a loveless marriage within a short time after the breakup. Of this period, Katey would later write: "My father was like a madman when my mother left home. . . . This affair brought out all that was worst—all that was weakest in him. He [seemingly] did not care what happened to any of us. *Nothing could surpass the misery and unhappiness of our home*" (Kaplan, p. 399, emphasis added).

Family life was never the same—for that matter, neither was Dickens. There was another woman: beautiful eighteen-year-old Ellen Ternan, who had performed in *The Frozen Deep* with him; but she never came to live at Gad's Hill. And sadly, Dickens forced many of their friends to take sides. In his treatment during this period of Catherine, his children, his extended family, and his friends, he exhibited an unbecoming ruthlessness and unkindness.

Certainly, all this unhappiness shortened his life. It definitely aged him.

Meanwhile, because of a change of publishers, Dickens changed the name of his magazine to *All the Year Round;* and because of his story serializations, its sales skyrocketed from 40,000 an issue to 300,000 during the next ten years.

The core idea for *A Tale of Two Cities* had come to Dickens during the torment of 1858, when his personal world appeared to be caving in on him. Somewhere between his disintegrating marriage and the vicarious sacrifice in *The Frozen Deep,* to say nothing of a new love, the story had come to him. For some years, Dickens had experienced recurring dreams of being a prisoner, manacled and behind walls—for that was how his marriage had seemed to him. And Paris was, next to London, perhaps his favorite city. He had learned French, and since his books had been translated into French, he was almost as well known there as he was in London. So, in the wrenching drama of *The Frozen Deep,* with one sister's tears cascading down on him, and the other, her heart in her eyes, standing to the side, with the whole Franklin party imprisoned in ice and dying there, Dr. Manette's long imprisonment in the Bastille and Sidney Carton's renunciation and great sacrifice amid the holocaust of the Terror was born. Johnson notes that Dickens had thought of his own life with Catherine as an iron-bound and stone-walled misery, weighed down by adamantine chains. It is not strange that in the fantasy from which imagination is born Dickens should dream of a prisoner bitterly immured for years and at last set free, and of a despairing love rising to a noble height of sacrifice. The story as a whole reflected Dickens's anguished sense of the grandeur of renunciation, his longing for the ultimate woman, and his rebellion against the imprisoning codes of society that inflicted the most hideous sufferings on mankind.

Dickens had wrestled with a number of possible titles for this story: *One of These Days, Buried Alive, The Thread of Gold, The Doctor of Beauvais.* But he was not really satisfied with any of them. There was quite a waiting period anyhow, for in the seismic shocks of the year, he had not been able to concentrate on writing at all.

He turned to his dear friend Carlyle for ideas. Carlyle's landmark *French Revolution* was one of the most significant historical works of the age, and Dickens drew heavily from it. Carlyle took him so seriously that he buried him in two cartloads of books from the London Library. "The more Dickens waded through them, however, the more he felt with amazed admiration that Carlyle had torn out their vitals and fused them into his fulminous masterpiece, which was aflame with the very essence of the conflagration" (Johnson, p. 479).

By March, Dickens's unerring sense of title appropriateness had brought him to *A Tale of Two Cities,* and with the door slammed on the title search, he was ready to go on. With an eye on profits, he decided to issue the story monthly as well as weekly.

By the time he reached "The Track of the Storm" section, Dickens was caught up in the action and whirled along like a chip carried aloft on the crest of a tidal wave: "The boiling cauldron of the Terror was a macrocosm filled with huge and flaming projections of his own raging emotions" (Johnson, p. 479). Dickens found it difficult to choose sides: "He pities the victims, but his deepest understanding is with a people driven mad. Though he sickens at the cruelty of mass murder, in his heart there is also a sympathy for these frenzied mobs, turned wolfish by oppression, that rises to a fierce exultation" (Johnson, p. 480).

As for the female protagonist, that portrait would not have been possible without Ellen Ternan. The story itself began as "Richard Wardour lay on the ground, dying, and seeing Ellen out of the corner of his eye." Even the description of Lucie Nanette is unquestionably a real-life description of Ellen. The two patriarchal figures, Dr. Manette and Jarvis Lorry, represent significant growth in Dickens's ability to construct more balanced father-figures.

The crackling electricity of the tale comes from the two men who love Lucie: Sydney Carton and Charles Darnay. According to Kaplan, they are both Dickens. Darnay, like Dickens, has renounced his family's past and is starting over. Carton, on the other hand, has wasted his life and feels semi-damned—and can be redeemed only through renunciation.

The opening lines are considered perhaps the greatest in all literature:

It was the best of times, it was the worst of times, it was the age of wisdom, it was the age of foolishness, it was the epoch of belief, it was the epoch of incredulity, it was the season of Light, it was the season of Darkness, it was the spring of hope, it was the winter of despair, we had everything before us, we had nothing before us, we were all going direct to heaven, we were all going the other way—in short, the period was so far like the present period, that some of its noisiest authorities insisted on its being received, for good or for evil, in the superlative degree of comparison only.

And how incredible the odds against such a beginning being tacked to one of the greatest book endings in all literature: "It is a far, far better thing that

I do than I have ever done; it is a far, far better rest that I go to than I have ever known."

As the story hit its stride and began to thunder into full speed, smashing into kindling anything that stood in its way, Dickens sighed with satisfaction: "'The best story I have written, [it] has greatly moved and excited me in the doing, and Heaven knows I have done my best and believed in it.' The public was dazzled by the sureness of style, the firmness of tone, the combination of literary qualities and noble feelings whose ultimate referent was the model of Christ" (Kaplan, p. 415).

At home—if it could be called that anymore—things were different. Dickens had imagined that if he could only sever the shackles that bound him to Catherine and capture his beautiful Ellen, he would be happy at last. Ruefully, he discovered that that was not to be true. Katey's wedding breakfast brought the reality home to him. She was lovely, all in white, but he felt certain she did not love Charles Allston Collins—very much a mama's boy (even at thirty-one). Her mother was not there; neither were her grandmothers—Georgina was the only member of the large Hogarth family attending. After the wedding breakfast, Katey came out, dressed for her honeymoon—in black (appropriately, as it turned out, since apparently there was to be no consummation). Before leaving, she cried bitterly on her father's shoulder. "When the house was quiet and empty, Mary [her father refused to permit her to marry the man she loved] found her father in Katey's bedroom alone. He was on his knees, sobbing, with his head buried in her wedding gown, 'But for me,' he wept brokenly, 'Katey would not have left home'" (Johnson, pp. 485–86; Kaplan, pp. 418–21).

Ten days after the bride in black left on her sad honeymoon, Dickens's brother Alfred died. He was thirty-eight, just as Fanny had been when she died. Although Dickens was the eldest, he would outlive all of his brothers. Of the two remaining brothers, one would die just past forty, and the other in his late forties.

When sales of *All the Year Round* began to drop, Dickens called an editorial caucus. What should be done? Obviously, what would help most would be another book to follow *A Tale of Two Cities*. He would title it *Great Expectations,* and it would be the same length as *Tale*.

Expectations is again autobiographical, although not nearly as much as was true with *David Copperfield*. But Pip's humiliation and griefs mirror those of Dickens as a child. Johnson maintains that "fundamentally, the novel is a reassessment of Dickens's own former subservience to false values" (Johnson,

p. 490). Paradoxically, Pip's "great expectations" have to do with his dream of one day living as a gentleman on someone else's money—without having to lift a finger himself; yet Dickens had nothing but scorn for the idle class, the aristocratic drones who made such messes of their lives.

Unquestionably, too, there is much in Pip's enslavement to Estella that mirrors Dickens's obsession with Ellen. Johnson maintains that "never before had he portrayed a man's love for a woman with such depth or revealed its desperation of compulsive suffering. David Copperfield's heartache for Dora is an iridescent dream-grief compared with Pip's nightmare reality. Pip's love is without illusion, all self-absorbed need [Victorian mores precluded Dickens from discussing sexuality other than in generalities]; his desire for Estella is as self-centered as his desire to be a gentleman. It is the culminating symbol and the crowning indictment of a society dedicated to selfish ends" (Johnson, pp. 490–91). But Johnson points out that Pip is not irredeemably selfish—as the story's conclusion reveals.

Kaplan insightfully notes that "unlike [Dickens's] previous orphan heroes . . . , Pip is utterly unheroic; unromanticized, his sensibility and moral code free of the complications of talent and authorial self-glorification. He is as close to the self stripped bare as Dickens could ever get" (Kaplan, pp. 432–33).

The early setting of the book is Dickens's Kentish childhood utopia. Also from his childhood is the hulking prison from which the convict escaped. According to Kaplan, before Dickens started the book, knowing it would be heavily autobiographical, he reread *David Copperfield* in order to avoid duplication—and was deeply affected by it. It helped that he was now living in the house he had once dreamed of owning and could look out on the setting of the book. Like *David Copperfield, Expectations* was narrated in first person. G. K. Chesterton declares that "he never wrote anything better, considered as literature, than the first chapters of *Great Expectations*" (*Britannica* VII, p. 334).

Meanwhile, Dickens's aging mother was becoming totally dependent on him. As for friendships, almost all of his early friends were dead, thus he felt more and more alone. Those who surrounded him now were mostly—as Johnson puts it—"literary dependants" (Johnson, p. 492).

Dickens began to spend more of his time giving public readings of his works. In those days of print dominance, for an author-elocutionist to read, with dramatic expression, from his works was as close to stage performances as one could get. Initially, it appears that Dickens went into it to test the waters, so to speak: to see if—after separating from Catherine—he had lost his following.

Clearly, those who thronged to his readings divorced their love for his books from any moral judgment of his private life.

Dickens could not have known it, but in *Our Mutual Friend* (written in 1864/65), he was writing his last complete full-length novel. It would be a book set in London—but a far cry from the joyous *Pickwick* of his youth. In a way, it was his *King Lear*, for, though only in his fifties, he had been battered beyond his years by the trauma in his life. In *Friend*, the great city of London cast somber shadows: It was "a hopeless city with no rent in the canopy of its sky." And, as Johnson points out, "the structure of society is one in which dominance has passed from the aristocracy to the middle class, capitalism, and the stock exchange. Money now seemed its only aim, pecuniary respectability its only standard" (Johnson, p. 497).

From all indications, Dickens had, over time, been able to persuade Ellen Ternan to come to Gad's Hill more often and to go places with him; but it brought neither of them much happiness, for both were torn by guilt and shame.

About this time, Dickens received a letter from a Jewish woman, Mrs. Eliza Davis, who told him "that Jews regarded his portrayal of Fagin in *Oliver Twist* as 'a great wrong' to their people" (Johnson, p. 504). Dickens hadn't really thought of it in that light before; so, to balance things out a bit, in his new book, he introduced Mr. Riah, "a gentle old man caught in the coils of a Christian moneylender" (Johnson, p. 505).

Meanwhile, an event occurred that jolted Dickens into apprehensions about the amount of time left to him. On June 9, 1865, he was with Mrs. Ternan and Ellen on a train from Dover to London when it crashed. All around them were mangled bodies and the cries of the wounded. Dickens climbed out of their train car, teetering precariously over a void, and helped all he could. Later he came back for the Ternans and for his precious manuscript, a segment of *Our Mutual Friend*. Ten passengers on the train—seven of them women—died, and forty were seriously wounded. Ellen's health was never the same afterward. Newspapers carried stories of the event, complete with names.

The emotional effect of the train wreck on Dickens can be seen in the story line and characters of *Our Mutual Friend*. Kaplan notes that "redemption . . . in *Our Mutual Friend* is a Christian affair in a frighteningly un-Christian culture. Material and psychological disintegration are constant threats—death by exploitation, death by brutalization, death by dehumanization, death by spiritual atrophy, death by one's body being inhabited by the materialism that the society promotes" (Kaplan, p. 474).

Kaplan feels that the character Bradley Headstone is perhaps "Dickens' most powerful negative self-portrait . . . the dark side of his own passion, willfulness, . . . creativity . . . and self-destructiveness" (Kaplan, pp. 474–75). Having completed the manuscript, Dickens resumed his public readings—this time, at an even more killing pace. For a while, he toyed with the idea of going to Australia, but finally decided against it. Now, the United States . . . that was another matter entirely: It was unfinished business. Friends and family alike tried to dissuade him from going, for his health was failing. After years of burning the candle at both ends, the middle had shrunk alarmingly. However, Dickens was promised £10,000 minimum (around US$2 million in today's purchasing power) to be deposited in a bank in England, if he would go. To Georgina and Mary, Dickens admitted, "I begin to feel myself drawn towards America, as Darnay in *A Tale of Two Cities* was attracted to the Loadstone Rock, Paris" (Johnson, p. 525).

No Relief But in Action

Dickens had always been a driven man, but about the mid-1860s, he took the governor off his engine and let her out. There was no one left in his life to challenge his absolute control—they could only weakly advise and wait for the inevitable accounting from a body and heart faithful, dependable, and resilient almost beyond belief.

Other than in his magazine, Dickens wrote little else. He did begin a new novel, *The Mystery of Edwin Drood,* but it remains a mystery to this day because he never completed it. Undoubtedly, he had finally decided to write a mystery because of his long association with Wilkie Collins, author of *The Woman in White* and *The Moonstone.*

As the time drew near for his second trip to the United States, Dickens began to have increasing trouble with his left foot, a physical problem dating back to the train wreck. His apprehension mounted: Should he go? Of course he would go—nothing short of death could stop him once he had made up his mind.

It was the evening of November 2, 1867, and excitement ran high in London's Freemason's Hall. Around 450 of the most distinguished men in the empire, and about 100 women, were there to pay tribute to Dickens, the greatest author of the age. According to Johnson, "wild enthusiasm greeted the arrival of the two most famous living novelists as Dickens entered on [Bulwer-]Lytton's arm. Following the procession were Lord Chief Justice Cockburn, the Lord Mayor of London, Lord Houghton, Sir Charles Russell, and an assemblage of the Royal Academicians" (Johnson, pp. 531–32).

In his tribute to Dickens, Bulwer-Lytton said, "Happy the man who makes clear his title-deeds to the royalty of genius while he yet lives. . . . Seldom, I say, has that kind of royalty been quietly conceded to any man of genius until his tomb becomes his throne, and yet there is not one of us now present who thinks it strange that it is granted without a murmur to the guest whom we receive tonight" (Johnson, p. 532). When Dickens rose to acknowledge the tribute, the audience lost control. "Men leaped on chairs, tossed up napkins, waved glasses and decanters above their heads. The ladies' gallery was a flag of waving hands and handkerchiefs. Colour and pallour followed each other in Dickens's face, and 'those wonderful eyes,' said one guest, 'flamed around like a search light'; tears streamed down his cheeks and as he tried to speak his voice faltered" (Johnson, p. 533). Though he eventually regained his composure and gave an eloquent response, many felt that the evening's climax was Dickens's silent tears.

Then it was time to say good-bye to his family—including farewell to Charley's children, his only grandchildren. When he came to little Mary Angela (whose nickname was "McKitty"), she—since he didn't like to be called "Grandfather"—hugged him and called him by her pet substitute name, "Wenerables." On November 9, 1867, Dickens left Liverpool and headed for America on the *Cuba*.

As it prepared for Dickens's arrival on November 19, the proud, aristocratic, staid city of Boston went into a frenzy—the streets were swept twice, and the capitol building and old South Church were repainted. And there were Dickens-related souvenirs everywhere—from "Little Nell Cigars" to "Pickwick Snuff." As the *Cuba*, its whistle shrieking, steamed into port, showers of rockets lit up the night sky. When Dickens disembarked, he was met by cheers and applause from thousands of people crowding the docks and streets. He was taken immediately to the Parker House, where George Dolby (his tour manager) told him the tickets for the first four readings were already gone, thanks to a line half a mile long. The next day, Longfellow arrived for a visit; later he brought Emerson, Holmes, and Agassiz with him as well.

Dickens quickly noted that much had changed since his last visit a quarter of a century before. For one thing, most people now respected his personal space. In his daily walks (seven to ten miles), whenever he'd stop to look in a window, the people nearby stopped, too.

A most poignant day was Thanksgiving, when he dined at the Craigie

House with Longfellow. In the bookshelves, he noted that there was a shelf of his own books, "and [he] said with a wink that delighted Longfellow's children, 'Ahh! I see you read the best authors!'" But throughout the meal and the visit, the house was haunted by the memory of Longfellow's beautiful wife whose dress had caught fire six years before: "She was in a blaze in an instant, rushed into his arms with a wild cry, and never spoke afterwards" (Johnson, p. 535). She died within hours, in agony.

After the initial Boston readings, Dickens shuffled between East Coast cities. New York went as crazy as Boston had in anticipation of Dickens's arrival: People stood—and slept on mattresses—in line all night, with 5,000 there by morning. And at Steinway Hall, the German janitor greeted Dickens with eloquence: "'Mr. Diggins . . . you are greed, meinherr. There is no ent to you.' Then, reopening the door and sticking his head out, 'Bedder and bedder,' he added; 'Wot negst'" (Johnson, p. 537).

Meanwhile, Dickens came down with a terrible cold, which plagued him the entire trip. But no matter how raw his throat was in the afternoon, somehow he always made it through the readings. A feel for these performances can be gained from the diary of laughing Allegra, Longfellow's twelve-year-old daughter:

> Sam Weller and Mr. Pickwick, Nicholas Nickleby and the old gentleman and the vegetable marrows over the garden wall. How he did make Aunt Betsy Trotwood snap out, "Janet, donkeys"—and David Copperfield yearn over the handsome sleeping Steerforth. How the audience loved best of all the *Christmas Carol* and how they laughed as Dickens fairly smacked his lips as there came the "smell like an eating house and a pastry cook's next door to each other, with a laundress's next door to that," as Mrs. Cratchit bore in the Christmas pudding, and how they nearly wept as Tiny Tim cried, "God bless us every one!" (Johnson, p. 538)

By now Dickens realized that, because of his ill health, he'd have to eliminate from his tour Chicago, St. Louis, and Cincinnati, which elicited howls of outrage from the Midwest. Dickens did find time to send $1,000 to Mrs. Clemm, Poe's mother-in-law, who had been suffering from need since Poe's death.

In Washington, President Andrew Johnson, the chief cabinet members, the Supreme Court, ambassadors, naval and military officers, government officials, politicians, and other dignitaries, all came the first night of his arrival, and many more came the following nights.

Even though the city was in an uproar over impeachment proceedings, President Johnson invited Dickens to call at the White House; later they also dined with statesman Charles Sumner and the just dismissed secretary of war Edwin Stanton. During their meal, the subject of Abraham Lincoln came up. Both Sumner and Stanton had attended a cabinet meeting the ill-fated day on which Lincoln had been assassinated, and they had been with him later as he died. Stanton, remembering that last cabinet meeting, called attention to the fact that the president—instead of lolling about as he usually did—was sitting erect in a dignified way and had told them of a recurring dream he had had: "I am on a great broad rolling river—and I am in a boat—and I drift!" (Kaplan, p. 523).

Dickens was visibly affected by the story and, for the rest of his life, he told it to anyone who would listen.

At the Delmonico farewell dinner in New York, Dickens came in, leaning on Horace Greeley's arm. At the end of the banquet, Dickens thanked the guests, telling them, with a smile, that he had learned a few things about America over the last twenty-five years, emphasizing that, on this visit, "I have been received with unsurpassable politeness, delicacy, sweet temper, hospitality, consideration, and . . . respect for . . . privacy" (Kaplan, p. 528).

There was a huge crowd to see him off on April 22. Dickens limped along, for his left foot was giving him increasing pain. The trip had far exceeded his financial expectations: £20,000 instead of £10,000.

Early in May 1868, as Dickens stepped off the Graveshead train and headed home, he saw that the houses on the way to Gad's Hill were bedecked with banners and flags and that people everywhere were welcoming him home.

In his last public readings, Dickens increasingly included death scenes. For a long time, he had included "The Death of Little Nell" and other moving passages. Now he added "The Murder of Nancy." In reading such passages, women often fainted. The act of reading them took a toll on him as well. Kaplan maintains that so total was Dickens's identification with the murder of Nancy by Sikes that afterward, on his way home, he'd guiltily look back to see if police were following to arrest him. During the readings, his pulse would rise from 72 to 112.

When Dickens finally went to his doctor to ask about the pain in his left foot and the fact that he would skip words or transpose them in his readings, among other things, he was told that he had probably experienced a minor stroke.

"No more readings!" commanded the doctor.

But Dickens couldn't live without them. Kaplan takes us to the last of Dickens's 450 or so readings, on March 15, 1870. "Tired, sad, his left foot in pain, the exhausted Prospero made his dreaded final appearance on the platform. He read *A Christmas Carol* and the trial scene from *Pickwick*. Against expectations, finding the energy to make one last effort, he read with verve and brilliance. The applause was overwhelming, and seemed to go on and on. Finally, it was quiet again" (Kaplan, p. 548). In the silent hall, Dickens confessed how he had just brought to an end fifteen years of performing. Then, gathering his strength, he concluded with these words: "'From these garish lights I now vanish evermore, with a heartfelt, respectful, and grateful farewell.' He walked slowly from the platform into the wings, as if in deep mourning. Tumultuous applause and handkerchief-waving brought him back one more time. Tears rolled down his cheeks. He kissed his hands to his friends, good-bye" (Kaplan, p. 549).

On March 9, Dickens had a private audience with Queen Victoria at Buckingham Palace. Instead of ten to fifteen minutes, it lasted close to an hour and a half. Dickens spoke of his latest works, his American tour, and Lincoln's dream; and they exchanged gifts—he gave her a copy of *David Copperfield*. Later, at other dinners, he chatted with Disraeli and Gladstone (considered by many to be two of the greatest prime ministers the British Empire has ever had).

The Mystery of Edwin Drood was Dickens's swan song. Had he lived to complete it, it would, for the first time, have told the story—obliquely, it is true—of Dickens's entire life. Kaplan maintains that the book is as autobiographical as *David Copperfield*.

Early in June 1870, Dickens was back at Gad's Hill. All around him were the sights and fragrances of early summer. The new conservatory had just been finished. Joking with Katey, he pronounced, "You now see POSITIVELY the last improvement on Gad's Hill" (Johnson, p. 578). And they laughed. On Sunday, he seemed refreshed when he returned from a quiet afternoon walk. "When dinner was over, he and Katey remained sitting in the dining room to be near the flowers in the conservatory, while they listened to Mary sing in the drawing room. At eleven o'clock, Mary and Georgina retired, but Dickens and Katey sat enjoying the warm perfumed night air. He and his daughter talked long and affectionately" (Johnson, p. 578). Then he told her that he wished he had been "a better father, and a better man"(Johnson, p. 578). Later he spoke of his hopes that he might make a success of *Edwin Drood*, "'if, please God, I live to finish it.' Katey looked startled. 'I say if,' Dickens told her, 'because you know, my dear child, I have not been strong lately'" (Johnson, p. 578). It was 3 A.M. before they finished talking.

Katey got up late that June 4 and went out to the recently built writing chalet to tell her father good-bye (she planned to be gone till Saturday). She felt uneasy and made Georgina promise to write her the next day to reassure her that her father was still all right. But as she waited for the carriage to be brought around, she felt she must go back to him. Much later, she would write of that moment: "His head was bent low down over his work, and he turned an eager and rather flushed face towards me as I entered." Usually, Dickens would merely raise his cheek for a good-bye kiss, say a few parting words, and go back to work. But not this time. When he saw her, "he pushed his chair back from the writing table, opened his arms, and took me into them." Then she hurried back to the house, saying to herself, without knowing why, *I am so glad I went—I am so glad* (Johnson, p. 579).

On Wednesday, June 6, uncharacteristically, Dickens wrote all day on the novel he would never finish. The last page he ever wrote depicts a hauntingly beautiful Rochester morning:

Changes of glorious light from morning boughs, songs of birds, scents from gardens, woods, and fields—or, rather, from the one great garden of the whole cultivated island in its yielding time—penetrate the Cathedral, subdue its earthly odour and preach of the Resurrection and the Life. The cold stone tombs of centuries ago grow warm; and flecks of brightness dart into the sternest marble corners of the buildings, fluttering there like wings. (Johnson, p. 579)

That night he intended to go to London. As he stood up to get ready, he started to fall, and Georgina helped to lower him to the floor. Doctors were sent for, and telegrams were sent to Mary, Katey, and others. Just before they had gone out for the evening, Katey had suddenly turned to Mary and said, "Mamie, I feel something is going to happen to us"(Johnson, p. 580).

Early the next morning, Charley and the London doctor arrived. The doctor pronounced it a paralytic stroke. Katey was sent to London to inform her mother, and Ellen was sent for, too. All day, members of the immediate family gathered.

"Just before six in the evening . . . Dickens's breathing grew fainter. At ten minutes past, he gave a deep sigh. His eyes were closed, but a tear welled from under his right eye and trickled down his cheek. Then he was gone. 'Like a weary factory child'" (Johnson, p. 580). He was fifty-eight.

The news of Dickens's death flashed around the world—across the vast reaches of the British Empire, to India, Australia, Canada, to the United States.

"I never knew an author's death to cause such general mourning. It is no exaggeration to say that the whole country is stricken with grief," wrote Longfellow.

In Genoa, a headline in the Italian newspaper read: *Nostro Carlo Dickens è Morto* [Our Charles Dickens Is Dead].

In the Parisian *Moniteur des Artes* were these words: "My pen trembles between my fingers at the thought of all that we—his family—have lost in Charles Dickens."

The bell of St. Stephens was just sounding nine-thirty when the procession (of three carriages only, as mandated in Dickens's will, with no public funeral, no public homage) reached the entrance to the Dean's Yard.

There was sudden silence.

Then the great bell of Westminster Abbey began to toll . . . and the vast city came to a complete halt.

Shortly afterward, at the command of the dean of Westminster (countermanding the injunction in Dickens's will), the massive doors of the great cathedral slowly opened to let the waiting people in.

And there, in Poets Corner—next to Handel, Macaulay, and Johnson, and not far from the busts and monuments of Milton, Spenser, Dryden, Chaucer, and Shakespeare—thousands of men, women, and children passed silently by Dickens's tomb, hour after hour, day after day—each leaving a flower and a tear. (The section on Dickens's death and funeral is derived from Johnson, pp. 571–83; Kaplan, pp. 553–56; and Tomlin, p. 42.)

Joseph Leininger Wheeler, Ph.D.
The Grey House
Conifer, Colorado

Works by Charles Dickens

Major Works

1836–1837	*Sketches by Boz: Illustrative of Every-Day Life and Every-Day People* *The Pickwick Papers*
1837–1839	*Oliver Twist* *Nicholas Nickleby*
1840–1841	*The Old Curiosity Shop* *Barnaby Rudge*
1842–1843	*American Notes*
1843–1844	*Martin Chuzzlewit* *A Christmas Carol*
1844	*The Chimes*
1846–1848	*The Battle of Life* *The Cricket on the Hearth* *The Haunted Man* *Dombey and Son* *Pictures from Italy*
1849–1850	*The Life of Our Lord* *David Copperfield*
1851–1853	*A Child's History of England*, Vols. 1 and 2
1854	*Hard Times*
1855–1857	*Little Dorrit*
1859–1861	*A Tale of Two Cities* *Great Expectations*
1864–1865	*Our Mutual Friend*
1870	*The Mystery of Edwin Drood* (incomplete)

Minor Works

1821   *Misnar: The Sultan of India*

1836   "The Strange Gentleman" (lyrics)
               "The Village Coquettes" (lyrics)
               Is She His Wife?

1838   *Memoirs of Grimaldi*
               Sketches of a Young Gentleman
               Gabriel Vardon: The Locksmith of London

1839   *Sketches of Young Couples*

1857   *Lazy Tour of Two Idle Apprentices*
               (with Wilkie Collins)

Magazines

Household Words

All the Year Round

MARLEY'S GHOST

---
[1] Used as "stanza" of a carol.

M arley was dead, to begin with. There is no doubt whatever about that. The register of his burial was signed by the clergyman, the clerk, the undertaker, and the chief mourner. Scrooge signed it. And Scrooge's name was good upon the Exchange for anything he chose to put his hand to. Old Marley was as dead as a doornail.

Mind! I don't mean to say that I know, of my own knowledge, what there is particularly dead about a doornail. I might have been inclined, myself, to regard a coffin nail as the deadest piece of ironmongery in the trade. But the wisdom of our ancestors is in the simile; and my unhallowed hands shall not disturb it, or the country's done for. You will, therefore, permit me to repeat, emphatically, that Marley was as dead as a doornail.

Scrooge knew he was dead? Of course he did. How could it be otherwise? Scrooge and he were partners for I don't know how many years. Scrooge was his sole executor, his sole administrator, his sole assign, his sole residuary legatee, his sole friend, and his sole mourner. And even Scrooge was not so dreadfully cut up by the sad event but that he was an excellent man of business on the very day of the funeral and solemnized it with an undoubted bargain.

The mention of Marley's funeral brings me back to the point I started from. There is no doubt that Marley was dead. This must be distinctly understood, or nothing wonderful can come of the story I am going to relate. If we were not perfectly convinced that Hamlet's father died before the play began, there would be nothing more remarkable in his taking a stroll at night, in an easterly wind, upon his own ramparts, than there would be in any other middle-aged gentleman rashly turning out after dark in a breezy spot—say St. Paul's churchyard, for instance—literally to astonish his son's weak mind.

Scrooge never painted out Old Marley's name. There it stood, years afterward, above the warehouse door: Scrooge and Marley. The firm was known as Scrooge and Marley. Sometimes people new to the business called Scrooge Scrooge, and sometimes Marley, but he answered to both names. It was all the same to him.

Oh, but he was a tightfisted hand at the grindstone, Scrooge! A squeezing, wrenching, grasping, scraping, clutching, covetous old sinner! Hard and sharp as flint, from which no steel had ever struck out generous fire; secret and self-contained, and solitary as an oyster. The cold within him froze his old features, nipped his pointed nose, shriveled his cheek, stiffened his gait; made his eyes red, his thin lips blue; and spoke out shrewdly in his grating voice. A frosty rime was on his head, and on his eyebrows, and on his wiry chin. He carried his own low temperature always about him; he iced his office in the dog days and didn't thaw it one degree at Christmas.

External heat and cold had little influence on Scrooge. No warmth could warm, no wintry weather chill him. No wind that blew was bitterer than he, no falling snow was more intent upon its purpose, no pelting rain less open to entreaty. Foul weather didn't know how to get at him. The heaviest rain, and snow, and hail, and sleet could boast of the advantage over him in only one respect. They often "came down" handsomely, and Scrooge never did.

Nobody ever stopped him in the street to say, with gladsome looks, "My dear Scrooge, how are you? When will you come to see me?" No beggars implored him to bestow a trifle, no children asked him what o'clock it was, no man or woman ever once in all his life inquired the way to such and such a place, of Scrooge. Even the blind men's dogs appeared to know him; and when they saw him coming, they would tug their owners into doorways and up courts; and then they would wag their tails as though they said, *No eye at all is better than an evil eye, dark master!*

But what did Scrooge care? It was the very thing he liked. To edge his way along the crowded paths of life, warning all human sympathy to keep its distance, was what the knowing ones call "nuts"[2] to Scrooge.

---

2 Agreeable, gratifying; a source of pleasure or delight.

Once upon a time—of all the good days in the year, on Christmas Eve— old Scrooge sat busy in his countinghouse. It was cold, bleak, biting weather; foggy withal; and he could hear the people in the court outside go wheezing up and down, beating their hands upon their breasts, and stamping their feet upon the pavement stones to warm them. The city clocks had only just gone three, but it was quite dark already—it had not been light all day—and candles were flaring in the windows of the neighboring offices, like ruddy smears upon the palpable brown air. The fog came pouring in at every chink and keyhole and was so dense without that, although the court was of the narrowest, the houses opposite were mere phantoms. To see the dingy cloud come drooping down, obscuring everything, one might have thought that nature lived close by and was brewing on a large scale.

The door of Scrooge's countinghouse was open so that he might keep his eye upon his clerk, who in a dismal little cell beyond, a sort of tank, was copying letters. Scrooge had a very small fire, but the clerk's fire was so very much smaller that it looked like one coal. But he couldn't replenish it, for Scrooge kept the coal box in his own room; and so surely as the clerk came in with the shovel, the master predicted that it would be necessary for them to part. Wherefore the clerk put on his long white scarf and tried to warm himself at the candle; in which effort, not being a man of strong imagination, he failed.

"A merry Christmas, Uncle! God save you!" cried a cheerful voice. It was the voice of Scrooge's nephew, who came upon him so quickly that this was the first intimation he had of his approach.

"Bah!" said Scrooge. "Humbug!"

He had so heated himself with rapid walking in the fog and frost, this nephew of Scrooge's, that he was all in a glow: His face was ruddy and handsome, his eyes sparkled, and his breath smoked again.

"Christmas a humbug, Uncle!" said Scrooge's nephew. "You don't mean that, I am sure."

"I do," said Scrooge. "Merry Christmas! What right have you to be merry? What reason have you to be merry? You're poor enough."

"Come, then," returned the nephew gaily. "What right have you to be dismal? What reason have you to be morose? You're rich enough."

Scrooge, having no better answer ready on the spur of the moment, said, "Bah!" again; and followed it up with "Humbug!"

"Don't be cross, Uncle!" said the nephew.

"What else can I be," returned the uncle, "when I live in such a world of fools as this? Merry Christmas! Out upon 'Merry Christmas'! What's

Christmastime to you but a time for paying bills without money; a time for finding yourself a year older and not an hour richer; a time for balancing your books and having every item in 'em through a round dozen of months presented dead against you? If I could work my will," said Scrooge indignantly, "every idiot who goes about with 'Merry Christmas' on his lips would be boiled with his own pudding and buried with a stake of holly through his heart. He should!"

"Uncle!" pleaded the nephew.

"Nephew!" returned the uncle sternly. "Keep Christmas in your own way, and let me keep it in mine."

"Keep it!" repeated Scrooge's nephew. "But you don't keep it."

"Let me leave it alone, then," said Scrooge. "Much good may it do you! Much good it has ever done you!"

"There are many things from which I might have derived good, by which I have not profited, I dare say," returned the nephew. "Christmas among the rest. But I am sure I have always thought of Christmastime, when it has come around—apart from the veneration due to its sacred name and origin, if anything belonging to it can be apart from that—as a good time; a kind, forgiving, charitable, pleasant time; the only time I know of, in the long calendar of the year, when men and women seem by one consent to open their shut-up hearts freely and to think of people below them as if they really were fellow passengers to the grave and not another race of creatures bound on other journeys. And therefore, Uncle, though it has never put a scrap of gold or silver in my pocket, I believe that it *has* done me good and *will* do me good; and I say, God bless it!"

The clerk in the tank involuntarily applauded. Becoming immediately sensible of the impropriety, he poked the fire and extinguished the last frail spark forever.

"Let me hear another sound from *you,*" said Scrooge, "and you'll keep your Christmas by losing your position!

"You're quite a powerful speaker, sir," he added, turning to his nephew. "I wonder you don't go into Parliament."

"Don't be angry, Uncle. Come! Dine with us tomorrow."

Scrooge said that he would see him—yes, indeed he did. He went the whole length of the expression and said that he would see him in that extremity[3] first.

"But why?" cried Scrooge's nephew. "Why?"

---

3 The *very* hot place, for those damned for their sins.

"Why did you get married?" asked Scrooge.

"Because I fell in love."

"Because you fell in love!" growled Scrooge, as if that were the only one thing in the world more ridiculous than a merry Christmas. "Good afternoon!"

"Nay, Uncle, but you never came to see me before that happened. Why give it as a reason for not coming now?"

"Good afternoon," said Scrooge.

"I want nothing from you; I ask nothing of you. Why cannot we be friends?"

"Good afternoon!" said Scrooge.

"I am sorry, with all my heart, to find you so resolute. We have never had any quarrel to which I have been a party. But I have made the trial in homage to Christmas, and I'll keep my Christmas humor to the last. So a merry Christmas, Uncle!"

"Good afternoon," said Scrooge.

"And a happy New Year!"

"Good afternoon!" said Scrooge.

His nephew left the room without an angry word, notwithstanding. He stopped at the outer door to bestow the greetings of the season on the clerk, who, cold as he was, was warmer than Scrooge; for he returned them cordially.

"There's another fellow," muttered Scrooge, who overheard him. "My clerk, with fifteen shillings a week and a wife and family, talking about a merry Christmas. I'll retire to Bedlam."[4]

This lunatic, in letting Scrooge's nephew out, had let two other people in. They were portly gentlemen, pleasant to behold, and now stood, with their hats off, in Scrooge's office. They had books and papers in their hands. They bowed to him.

"Scrooge and Marley's, I believe," said one of the gentlemen, referring to his list. "Have I the pleasure of addressing Mr. Scrooge or Mr. Marley?"

"Mr. Marley has been dead these seven years," Scrooge replied. "He died seven years ago, this very night."

"We have no doubt his liberality is well represented by his surviving partner," said the gentleman, presenting his credentials.

It certainly was: for they had been two kindred spirits. At the ominous word "liberality," Scrooge frowned, shook his head, and handed the credentials back.

---

4 A famous London insane asylum.

"At this festive season of the year, Mr. Scrooge," said the gentleman, taking up a pen, "it is more than usually desirable that we should make some slight provision for the poor and destitute, who suffer greatly at the present time. Many thousands are in want of common necessaries; hundreds of thousands are in want of common comforts, sir."

"Are there no prisons?" asked Scrooge.

"Plenty of prisons," said the gentleman, laying down the pen again.

"And the Union workhouses?" demanded Scrooge. "Are they still in operation?"

"They are. Still," returned the gentleman, "I wish I could say they were not."

"The Treadmill and the Poor Law are in full vigor, then?" said Scrooge.

"Both very busy, sir."

"Oh! I was afraid, from what you said at first, that something had occurred to stop them in their useful course," said Scrooge. "I am very glad to hear it."

"Under the impression that they scarcely furnish Christian cheer of mind or body to the multitude," returned the gentleman, "a few of us are endeavoring to raise a fund to buy the poor some meat and drink and means of warmth. We choose this time, because it is a time, of all others, when Want is keenly felt and Abundance rejoices. What shall I put you down for?"

"Nothing!" Scrooge replied.

"You wish to be anonymous?"

"I wish to be left alone," said Scrooge. "Since you ask me what I wish, gentlemen, that is my answer. I don't make merry myself at Christmas, and I can't afford to make idle people merry. I help to support the establishments I have mentioned—they cost enough: And those who are badly off must go there."

"Many can't go there; and many would rather die."

"If they would rather die," said Scrooge, "they had better do it and decrease the surplus population. Besides—excuse me—I don't know that."

"But you might know it," observed the gentleman.

"It's not my business," Scrooge returned. "It's enough for a man to understand his own business and not to interfere with other people's. Mine occupies me constantly. Good afternoon, gentlemen!"

Seeing clearly that it would be useless to pursue their point, the gentlemen withdrew. Scrooge resumed his labors with an improved opinion of himself and in a more facetious temper than was usual with him.

Meanwhile, the fog and darkness thickened so, that people ran about with flaring torches, proffering their services to go before horses in carriages and conduct them on their way. The ancient tower of a church, whose gruff old bell was always peeping slyly down at Scrooge out of a Gothic window in the wall, became invisible and struck the hours and quarters in the clouds, with tremulous vibrations afterward, as if its teeth were chattering in its frozen head up there. The cold became intense. In the main street, at the corner of the court, some laborers were repairing the gas pipes and had lighted a great fire in a brazier, around which a party of ragged men and boys were gathered: warming their hands and winking their eyes before the blaze in rapture. The water plug being left in solitude, its overflowings suddenly congealed and turned to misanthropic ice. The brightness of the shops, where holly sprigs and berries crackled in the lamp heat of the windows, made pale faces ruddy as they passed. Poulterers' and grocers' trades became a splendid joke: a glorious pageant, with which it was next to impossible to believe that such dull principles as bargain and sale had anything to do. The lord mayor, in the stronghold of the mighty Mansion House, gave orders to his fifty cooks and butlers to keep Christmas as a lord mayor's household should; and even the little tailor, whom he had fined five shillings on the previous Monday for being drunk and bloodthirsty in the streets, stirred up tomorrow's puddings in his garret, while his lean wife and the baby sallied out to buy the beef.

Foggier yet, and colder! Piercing, searching, biting cold. If the good St. Dunstan[5] had but nipped the Evil Spirit's nose with a touch of such weather as that, instead of using his familiar weapons, then indeed he would have roared to lusty purpose. The owner of one scant young nose, gnawed and mumbled[6] by the hungry cold as bones are gnawed by the dogs, stooped down at Scrooge's keyhole to regale him with a Christmas carol; but at the first sound of

> God bless you, merry gentleman,
>
> May nothing you dismay!

Scrooge seized the ruler with such energy of action that the singer fled in terror, leaving the keyhole to the fog and even more congenial frost.

At length, the hour of shutting up the countinghouse arrived. With an ill will, Scrooge dismounted from his stool and tacitly admitted the fact to the expectant clerk in the tank, who instantly snuffed his candle out and put on his hat.

---

5 An English monk who, according to legend, once grabbed hold of the devil's nose with red-hot pincers.

6 Bit gently, with mouth closed.

"You'll want all day tomorrow, I suppose?" said Scrooge.

"If quite convenient, sir."

"It's not convenient," said Scrooge, "and it's not fair. If I was to stop half a crown for it, you'd think yourself ill used, I'll be bound."

The clerk smiled faintly.

"And yet," said Scrooge, "you don't think *me* ill used when I pay a day's wages for no work."

The clerk observed that it was only once a year.

"A poor excuse for picking a man's pocket every twenty-fifth of December!" said Scrooge, buttoning his greatcoat to the chin. "But I suppose you *must* have the whole day. Be here all the earlier next morning."

The clerk promised that he would; and Scrooge walked out with a growl. The office was closed in a twinkling, and the clerk, with the long ends of his white scarf dangling below his waist (for he boasted no greatcoat), went down a slide on Cornhill, at the end of a lane of boys, twenty times, in honor of its being Christmas Eve, and then ran home to Camden Town as hard as he could pelt, to play at blindman's buff.

Scrooge took his melancholy dinner in his usual melancholy tavern; and having read all the newspapers and beguiled the rest of the evening with his banker's book, he went home to bed. He lived in chambers that had once belonged to his deceased partner. They were a gloomy suite of rooms, in a lowering pile of building up a yard, where it had so little business to be that one could scarcely help fancying it must have run there when it was a young house, playing at hide-and-seek with other houses, and have forgotten the way out again. It was old enough now, and dreary enough, for nobody lived in it but Scrooge: the other rooms being all let out as offices. The yard was so dark that even Scrooge, who knew its every stone, was fain to grope with his hands. The fog and frost so hung about the black old gateway of the house that it seemed as if the Genius of the Weather[7] sat in mournful meditation on the threshold.

Now, it is a fact that there was nothing at all particular about the knocker on the door, except that it was very large. It is also a fact that Scrooge had seen it, night and morning, during his whole residence in that place; also that Scrooge had as little of what is called fancy about him as any man in the City of London, even including—which is a bold word—the corporation, aldermen, and livery. Let it also be borne in mind that Scrooge had not bestowed one thought on Marley since his last mention of his seven-years-

---

7 Guardian, attendant spirit, or clerk, of the weather.

dead partner that afternoon. And then let any man explain to me, if he can, how it happened that Scrooge, having his key in the lock of the door, saw in the knocker, without its undergoing any intermediate process of change—not a knocker, but Marley's face.

Marley's face. It was not in impenetrable shadow, as the other objects in the yard were, but had a dismal light about it, like a bad lobster in a dark cellar. It was not angry or ferocious, but looked at Scrooge as Marley used to look: with ghostly spectacles turned up on its ghostly forehead. The hair was curiously stirred, as if by breath or hot air; and, though the eyes were wide open, they were perfectly motionless. That, and its livid color, made it horrible; but its horror seemed to be in spite of the face, and beyond its control, rather than a part of its own expression.

As Scrooge looked fixedly at this phenomenon, it was a knocker again.

To say that he was not startled, or that his blood was not conscious of a terrible sensation to which it had been a stranger from infancy, would be untrue. But he put his hand upon the key he had relinquished, turned it sturdily, walked in, and lighted his candle.

He *did* pause, with a moment's irresolution, before he shut the door; and he *did* look cautiously behind it first, as if he half-expected to be terrified with the sight of Marley's pigtail sticking out into the hall. But there was nothing on the back of the door, except the screws and nuts that held the knocker on: So he said, "Pooh, pooh!" and closed it with a bang.

The sound resounded through the house like thunder. Every room above, and every cask in the wine merchant's cellars below, appeared to have a separate peal of echoes of its own. Scrooge was not a man to be frightened by echoes. He fastened the door and walked across the hall and up the stairs slowly, trimming his candle as he went.

You may talk vaguely about driving a coach-and-six up a good old flight of stairs, or through a bad young Act of Parliament; but I mean to say you might have got a hearse up that staircase and taken it broadwise, with the splinter bar[8] toward the wall and the door toward the balustrades, and done it easily. There was plenty of width for that, and room to spare; which is perhaps the reason why Scrooge thought he saw a locomotive hearse going on before him in the gloom. Half a dozen gas lamps out of the street wouldn't have lighted the entry too well, so you may suppose that it was pretty dark with just Scrooge's candle.

Up Scrooge went, not caring a button for that. Darkness is cheap, and

---

8 Front crossbar that supports the springs.

Scrooge liked it. But before he shut his heavy door, he walked through his rooms to see that all was right. He had just enough recollection of the face to desire to do that.

Sitting room, bedroom, lumber room.[9] All as they should be. Nobody under the table, nobody under the sofa; a small fire in the grate; spoon and basin ready; and the little saucepan of gruel (Scrooge had a cold in his head) upon the hob. Nobody under the bed, nobody in the closet; nobody in his dressing gown, which was hanging up in a suspicious attitude against the wall. Lumber room as usual. Old fireguard, old shoes, two fish baskets, washing stand on three legs, and a poker.

Quite satisfied, he closed his door and locked himself in—double locked himself in, which was not his custom. Thus secured against surprise, he took off his cravat; put on his dressing gown, slippers, and nightcap; and sat down before the fire to take his gruel.

It was a very low fire indeed; nothing on such a bitter night. He was obliged to sit close to it, and brood over it, before he could extract the least sensation of warmth from such a handful of fuel. The fireplace was an old one, built by some Dutch merchant long ago, and paved all around with quaint Dutch tiles designed to illustrate the Scriptures. There were Cains and Abels, Pharaoh's daughters, Queens of Sheba, angelic messengers descending through the air on clouds like feather beds, Abrahams, Belshazzars, apostles putting off to sea in butter boats, hundreds of figures to attract his thoughts; and yet that face of Marley, seven years dead, came like the ancient prophet's rod and swallowed up the whole. If each smooth tile had been a blank at first, with power to shape some picture on its surface from the disjointed fragments of his thoughts, there would have been a copy of old Marley's head on every one.

"Humbug!" said Scrooge, and he walked across the room.

After several turns, he sat down again. As he threw his head back in the chair, his glance happened to rest upon a bell, a disused bell, that hung in the room and communicated, for some purpose now forgotten, with a chamber in the highest story of the building. It was with great astonishment, and with a strange, inexplicable dread, that, as he looked, he saw this bell begin to swing. It swung so softly in the outset that it scarcely made a sound; but soon it rang out loudly, and so did every bell in the house.

This might have lasted half a minute, or a minute, but it seemed an hour. The bells ceased, as they had begun, together. They were succeeded by a

---

[9] A room used for firewood and general storage.

clanking noise deep down below as if some person were dragging a heavy chain over the casks in the wine-merchant's cellar. Scrooge then remembered to have heard that ghosts in haunted houses were described as dragging chains.

The cellar door flew open with a booming sound, and then he heard the noise much louder on the floors below; then coming up the stairs; then coming straight toward his door.

"It's humbug still!" said Scrooge. "I won't believe it."

His color changed, though, when, without a pause, it came on through the heavy door and passed into the room before his eyes. Upon its coming in, the dying flame leaped up, as though it cried, "I know him! Marley's Ghost!" and fell again.

The same face: the very same. Marley in his pigtail, usual waistcoat, tights, and boots; the tassels on the latter bristling, like his pigtail, and his coat skirts, and the hair upon his head. The chain he drew was clasped about his middle. It was long and wound about him like a tail; and it was made (for Scrooge observed it closely) of cash boxes, keys, padlocks, ledgers, deeds, and heavy purses wrought in steel. His body was transparent, so that Scrooge, observing him and looking through his waistcoat, could see the two buttons on his coat behind.

Scrooge had often heard it said that Marley had no bowels,[10] but he had never believed it until now.

No, nor did he believe it even now. Though he looked the Phantom through and through and saw it standing before him; though he felt the chilling influence of its death-cold eyes and marked the very texture of the folded kerchief bound about its head and chin, which wrapper he had not observed before, he was still incredulous and fought against his senses.

"How now!" said Scrooge, caustic and cold as ever. "What do you want with me?"

"Much!" Marley's voice, no doubt about it.

"Who are you?"

"Ask me who I *was.*"

"Who *were* you, then?" said Scrooge, raising his voice. "You're particular— for a shade."[11] He was going to say "*to* a shade," but subsituted this as more appropriate.

"In life I was your partner, Jacob Marley."

---

[10] At one time, bowels were thought to be the seat of compassion—see 1 John 3:17 (King James).

[11] A ghost; a degree.

Marley's Ghost

"Can you—can you sit down?" asked Scrooge, looking doubtfully at him.

"I can."

"Do it, then."

Scrooge asked the question, because he didn't know whether a ghost so transparent might find himself in a condition to take a chair; and he felt that in the event of its being impossible, it might involve the necessity of an embarrassing explanation. But the Ghost sat down on the opposite side of the fireplace, as if he were quite used to it.

"You don't believe in me," observed the Ghost.

"I don't," said Scrooge.

"What evidence would you have of my reality, beyond that of your own senses?"

"I don't know," said Scrooge.

"Why do you doubt your senses?"

"Because," said Scrooge, "a little thing[12] affects them. A slight disorder of the stomach makes them cheats. You may be an undigested bit of beef, a blot of mustard, a crumb of cheese, a fragment of an underdone potato. There's more of gravy than of grave about you, whatever you are!"

Scrooge was not much in the habit of cracking jokes, nor did he feel, in his heart, by any means waggish then. The truth is that he tried to be smart, as a means of distracting his own attention and keeping down his terror: for the specter's voice disturbed the very marrow in his bones.

To sit staring at those fixed, glazed eyes in silence, for a moment, would play, Scrooge felt, the very deuce with him. There was something very awful, too, in the specter's being provided with an infernal atmosphere of his own. Scrooge could not feel it himself, but this was clearly the case. For though the ghost sat perfectly motionless, its hair, skirts, and tassels were still agitated as by the hot vapor from an oven.

"You see this toothpick?" asked Scrooge, returning quickly to the charge, for the reason just assigned; and wishing, though it were only for a second, to divert the vision's stony gaze from himself.

"I do," replied the Ghost.

"You are not looking at it," said Scrooge.

"But I see it," said the Ghost, "notwithstanding."

"Well!" returned Scrooge. "I have but to swallow this, and be for the rest of my days persecuted by a legion of goblins, all of my own creation. Humbug, I

---

[12] It was believed that dreams—and ghosts—were often induced by indigestion (in effect, hallucinations).

tell you—humbug!"

At this, the Spirit raised a frightful cry and shook its chain with such a dismal and appalling noise that Scrooge held on tightly to his chair, to save himself from falling in a swoon. But how much greater was his horror when the Phantom, taking off the bandage around its head, as if it were too warm to wear indoors, released its lower jaw, which dropped[13] down upon its breast!

Scrooge fell upon his knees and clasped his hands before his face.

"Mercy!" he said. "Dreadful apparition, why do you trouble me?"

"Man of the worldly mind," replied the Ghost, "do you believe in me or not?"

"I do," said Scrooge. "I must. But why do spirits walk the earth, and why do they come to me?"

"It is required of every man," the Ghost returned, "that the spirit within him should walk abroad among his fellowmen and travel far and wide; and if that spirit goes not forth in life, it is condemned to do so after death. It is doomed to wander through the world—oh, woe is me!—and witness what it cannot share, but might have shared on earth and turned to happiness!"

Again the specter raised a cry and shook its chain and wrung its shadowy hands.

"You are fettered," said Scrooge, trembling. "Tell me why."

"I wear the chain I forged in life," replied the Ghost. "I made it link by link, and yard by yard; I girded it on of my own free will, and of my own free will I wore it. Is its pattern strange to *you?*"

Scrooge trembled more and more.

"Or would you know," pursued the Ghost, "the weight and length of the strong coil you bear yourself? It was full as heavy and as long as this seven Christmas Eves ago. You have labored on it since. It is a ponderous chain!"

Scrooge glanced about him on the floor, in the expectation of finding himself surrounded by some fifty or sixty fathoms of iron cable. But he could see nothing.

"Jacob!" he said imploringly. "Old Jacob Marley, tell me more! Speak comfort to me, Jacob!"

"I have none to give," the host replied. "It comes from other regions,[14] Ebenezer Scrooge, and is conveyed by other ministers, to other kinds of men.

---

[13] The dead were often bound around the chin and head to keep the mouth closed.

[14] According to Hearn, Dickens was influenced here by Dante: Just as the poet Virgil is the guide to the poet Dante, just so the miser Marley is the guide to the miser Scrooge. Both visions apparently took place over a three-day period (Dante's at Easter, Scrooge's at Christmas). In Dante's Fourth Circle, the avaricious are condemned to roll great weights, hence Marley's similar punishment. As with Dante, both spirits speak in "veiled speech," as Christ cannot be spoken of in the infernal world.

Scrooge's Lookout

Nor can I tell you what I would. A very little more is all permitted to me. I cannot rest, I cannot stay, I cannot linger anywhere. My spirit never walked beyond our countinghouse—mark me!—in life my spirit never roved beyond the narrow limits of our money-changing hole; and weary journeys lie before me!"

It was a habit with Scrooge, whenever he became thoughtful, to put his hands in his breeches' pockets. Pondering on what the Ghost had said, he did so now, but without lifting up his eyes or getting off his knees.

"You must have been very slow about it, Jacob," Scrooge observed in a businesslike manner, though with humility and deference.

"Slow!" the Ghost repeated.

"Seven years dead," mused Scrooge. "And traveling all the time?"

"The whole time," said the Ghost. "No rest, no peace. Incessant torture of remorse."

"You travel fast?" asked Scrooge.

"On the wings of the wind," replied the Ghost.

"You might have got over a great quantity of ground in seven years," said Scrooge.

The Ghost, on hearing this, set up another cry and clanked its chain so hideously in the dead silence of the night that the ward[15] would have been justified in indicting it for a nuisance.

"O blind man, blind man!"[16] cried the Phantom. "Not to know that ages of incessant labor, by immortal creatures, for this earth must pass into eternity before the good of which it is susceptible is all developed! Not to know that any Christian spirit working kindly in its little sphere, whatever it may be, will find its mortal life too short for its vast means of usefulness! Not to know that no space of regret can make amends for one life's opportunities misused! Yet such was I! Oh, such was I!"

"But you were always a good man of business, Jacob," faltered Scrooge, who now began to apply this to himself.

"Business!" cried the Ghost, wringing its hands again. "Mankind was my business. The common welfare was my business; charity, mercy, forbearance, and benevolence were all my business. The dealings of my trade were but a drop of water in the comprehensive ocean of my business!"

---

15 An officer, watchman, or policeman of the ward (26 wards or parishes in London at that time, according to Hearn).

16 Hearn notes that Dickens was dissatisfied with the "Oh! Captive, bound, and double-ironed!" line and hence substituted these words in his later public readings.

It held up its chain at arm's length, as if that were the cause of all its unavailing grief, and flung it heavily upon the ground again.

"At this time of the rolling year," the specter said, "I suffer most. Why did I walk through crowds of fellow-beings with my eyes turned down and never raise them to that blessed star that led the Wise Men to a poor abode? Were there no poor homes to which its light would have conducted *me?*"

Scrooge was very much dismayed to hear the specter going on at this rate, and he began to quake exceedingly.

"Hear me!" cried the Ghost. "My time is nearly gone."

"I will," said Scrooge. "But don't be hard upon me! Don't be flowery, Jacob! Pray!"

"How it is that I appear before you in a shape that you can see, I may not tell. I have sat invisible beside you many and many a day."

It was not an agreeable idea. Scrooge shivered and wiped the perspiration from his brow.

"That is no light part of my penance," pursued the Ghost. "I am here tonight to warn you: that you have yet a chance and hope of escaping my fate. A chance and hope of my procuring, Ebenezer."

"You were always a good friend to me," said Scrooge. "Thank'ee!"

"You will be haunted," resumed the Ghost, "by three spirits."

Scrooge's countenance fell almost as low as the Ghost's had done.

"Is that the chance and hope you mentioned, Jacob?" he demanded in a faltering voice.

"It is."

"I—I think I'd rather not," said Scrooge.

"Without their visits," said the Ghost, "you cannot hope to shun the path I tread. Expect the first tomorrow when the bell tolls one."

"Couldn't I take 'em all at once and have it over with, Jacob?" hinted Scrooge.

"Expect the second on the next night at the same hour. The third, upon the next night when the last stroke of twelve has ceased to vibrate. Look to see me no more; and, for your own sake, remember what has passed between us!"

When it had said these words, the specter took its wrapper from the table and bound it around its head as before. Scrooge knew this by the smart sound its teeth made when the jaws were brought together by the bandage. He ventured to raise his eyes again and found his supernatural visitor confronting him in an erect attitude, with its chain wound over and about its arm.

The apparition walked backward from him; and, at every step it took, the window raised itself a little, so that when the specter reached it, it was wide open. It beckoned Scrooge to approach, which he did. When they were within two paces of each other, Marley's Ghost held up its hand, warning him to come no nearer. Scrooge stopped—not so much in obedience as in surprise and fear. For, on the raising of the hand, he became sensible of confused noises in the air; incoherent sounds of lamentation and regret; wailings inexpressibly sorrowful and self-accusatory. The specter, after listening for a moment, joined in the mournful dirge and floated out upon the bleak, dark night.

Scrooge followed to the window, desperate in his curiosity. He looked out.

The air was filled with phantoms, wandering hither and thither in restless haste, and moaning as they went. Every one of them wore chains like Marley's Ghost; some few (they might be guilty governments) were linked together; none were free. Many had been personally known to Scrooge in their lives. He had been quite familiar with one old ghost in a white waistcoat, with a monstrous iron safe attached to its ankle, who cried piteously at being unable to assist a wretched woman with an infant, whom it saw below upon a doorstep. The misery with them all was, clearly, that they sought to interfere, for good, in human matters and had lost the power forever.

Whether these creatures faded into mist, or mist enshrouded them, he could not tell. But they and their spirit voices faded together; and the night became as it had been when he walked home.

Scrooge closed the window and examined the door by which the Ghost had entered. It was double-locked, as he had locked it with his own hands, and the bolts were undisturbed. He tried to say "Humbug!" but stopped at the first syllable. And being, from the emotion he had undergone, or the fatigues of the day, or his glimpse of the Invisible World, or the monotone conversation of the Ghost, or the lateness of the hour, much in need of repose, he went straight to bed without undressing and fell asleep upon the instant.

THE FIRST OF THE THREE SPIRITS

When Scrooge awoke, it was so dark that, looking out of bed, he could scarcely distinguish the transparent window from the opaque walls of his chamber. He was endeavoring to pierce the darkness with his ferret eyes, when the chimes of a neighboring church [1] struck the four quarters. So he listened for the hour.

To his great astonishment, the heavy bell went on from six to seven, and from seven to eight, and regularly up to twelve; then stopped. Twelve! It was past two when he went to bed. The clock was wrong. An icicle must have got into the works. Twelve!

He touched the spring of his repeater, [2] to correct this most preposterous clock. Its rapid little pulse beat twelve and stopped.

"Why, it isn't possible," said Scrooge, "that I can have slept through a whole day and far into another night. It isn't possible that anything has happened to the sun, and this is twelve at noon!"

The idea being an alarming one, he scrambled out of bed, and groped his way to the window. He was obliged to rub the frost off with the sleeve of his dressing gown before he could see anything; and he could see very little then.

---

[1] According to Hearn's research (referencing Gwen Majors): St. Andrews Undershaft Church, at the corner of Leadenhall Street and St. Mary Avenue.

[2] Repeating watch or clock (invented about 1676).

All he could make out was that it was still very foggy and extremely cold, and that there was no noise of people running to and fro and making a great stir, as there unquestionably would have been if night had beaten off bright day and taken possession of the world. This was a great relief, because "three days after sight of this First of Exchange pay to Mr. Ebenezer Scrooge or his order,"[3] and so forth, would have become a mere United States security[4] if there were no days to count by.

Scrooge went to bed again, and thought, and thought, and thought it over and over, and could make nothing of it. The more he thought, the more perplexed he was; and the more he endeavored not to think, the more he thought.

Marley's Ghost bothered him exceedingly. Every time he resolved within himself, after mature inquiry, that it was all a dream, his mind flew back again, like a strong spring released, to its first position and presented the same problem to be worked all through: *Was it a dream or not?*

Scrooge lay in this state until the chime had gone three-quarters more, when he remembered, all of a sudden, that the Ghost had warned him of a visitation when the bell tolled one. He resolved to lie awake until the hour was passed; and, considering that he could no more go to sleep than go to heaven, this was perhaps the wisest resolution in his power.

The quarter was so long that he was more than once convinced he must have sunk into a doze unconsciously and missed the clock. At length, it broke upon his listening ear.

"Ding, dong!"

"A quarter past," said Scrooge, counting.

"Ding, dong!"

"Half past," said Scrooge.

"Ding, dong!"

"A quarter to it," said Scrooge.

"Ding, dong!"

"The hour itself," said Scrooge triumphantly, "and nothing else!"

He spoke before the hour bell sounded, which it now did with a deep, dull, hollow, melancholy ONE. Light flashed up in the room upon the instant, and the curtains of his bed were drawn.

---

[3] If a bill of exchange was not presented by the third day, it would not be honored, and the money would consequently be lost.

[4] After the Panic of 1837, many states repudiated their bonds, thus dramatically weakening American credit around the world.

The curtains of his bed were drawn aside, I tell you, by a hand. Not the curtains at his feet, nor the curtains at his back, but those to which his face was addressed. The curtains of his bed were drawn aside; and Scrooge, starting up into a half-recumbent attitude, found himself face-to-face with the unearthly visitor who drew them: as close to it as I am now to you, and I am standing in the spirit at your elbow.

It was a strange figure[5]—like a child; yet not so like a child as like an old man, viewed through some supernatural medium, which gave him the appearance of having receded from the view and being diminished to a child's proportions. Its hair, which hung about its neck and down its back, was white, as if with age; and yet the face had not a wrinkle in it, and the tenderest bloom was on the skin. The arms were very long and muscular; the hands the same, as if its hold were of uncommon strength. Its legs and feet, most delicately formed, were, like those upper members, bare. It wore a tunic of the purest white; and around its waist was bound a lustrous belt, the sheen of which was beautiful. It held a branch of fresh green holly in its hand; and, in singular contradiction of that wintry emblem, had its dress trimmed with summer flowers. But the strangest thing about it was that from the crown of its head there sprang a bright clear jet of light, by which all this was visible; and which was doubtless the occasion of its using, in its duller moments, a great extinguisher[6] for a cap, which it now held under its arm.

Even this, though, when Scrooge looked at it with increasing steadiness, was *not* its strangest quality. For, as its belt sparkled and glittered, now in one part and now in another, and what was light one instant at another time was dark, so the figure itself fluctuated in its distinctness: being now a thing with one arm, now with one leg, now with twenty legs, now a pair of legs without a head, now a head without a body—of which dissolving parts no outline would be visible in the dense gloom wherein they melted away. And, in the very wonder of this, it would be itself again: distinct and clear as ever.

"Are you the Spirit, sir, whose coming was foretold to me?" asked Scrooge.
"I am!"

The voice was soft and gentle; singularly low, as if, instead of being so close behind him, it were at a distance.

"Who and what are you?" Scrooge demanded.

---

[5] Hearn feels the reason for Leech's not illustrating the First Spirit was because Dickens was so ambiguous about it himself: More than 2,000 years old but young, like the Germanic *Christkindl*, or *Christkind*, which is usually portrayed by a girl; but if *Kris Kringle*, more an older man, such as St. Nicholas or Santa Claus.

[6] That there is need for an extinguisher implies a candlelike figure.

"I am the Ghost of Christmas Past."

"Long past?" inquired Scrooge, observant of its dwarfish stature.

"No. Your past."

Perhaps Scrooge could not have told anybody why, if anybody could have asked him; but he had a special desire to see the Spirit in its cap and begged it to be covered.

"What!" exclaimed the Ghost. "Would you so soon put out, with worldly hands, the light I give? Is it not enough that you are one of those whose passions made this cap and force me through whole trains of years to wear it low upon my brow?"

Scrooge reverently disclaimed all intention to offend or any knowledge of having willfully "bonneted"[7] the Spirit at any period of his life. He then made bold to inquire what business brought it there.

"Your welfare!" said the Ghost.

Scrooge expressed himself much obliged, but could not help thinking that a night of unbroken rest would have been more conducive to that end.

The Spirit must have heard him thinking, for it said immediately, "Your reclamation, then. Take heed!"

It put out its strong hand as it spoke and clasped him gently by the arm.

"Rise and walk with me!"

It would have been in vain for Scrooge to plead that the weather and the hour were not adapted to pedestrian purposes; that his bed was warm, and the thermometer a long way below freezing; that he was clad but lightly in his slippers, dressing gown, and nightcap; and that he had a cold upon him at that time. The grasp, though gentle as a woman's hand, was not to be resisted. He rose, but, finding that the Spirit made toward the window, clasped its robe in supplication.

"I am a mortal," Scrooge remonstrated, "and liable to fall."

"Bear but a touch of my hand *there*," said the Spirit, laying it upon his heart, "and you shall be upheld in more than this!"

As the words were spoken, they passed through the wall and stood upon an open country road, with fields on either hand. The city had entirely vanished. Not a vestige of it was to be seen. The darkness and the mist had vanished with it, for it was a clear, cold winter day, with snow upon the ground.

"Good Heaven!" said Scrooge, clasping his hands together as he looked about him. "I was bred in this place. I was a boy here!"

---

7 A pun with a double meaning: both knocking someone's hat down over the eyes or snuffing out a candle with a bonnet (or cap).

The Spirit gazed upon him mildly. Its gentle touch, though it had been light and instantaneous, appeared still present to the old man's sense of feeling. He was conscious of a thousand odors floating in the air, each one connected with a thousand thoughts, and hopes, and joys, and cares long, long forgotten!

"Your lip is trembling," said the Ghost. "And what is that upon your cheek?"

Scrooge muttered, with an unusual catching in his voice, that it was a tear; and begged the Ghost to lead him where it would.

"You recollect the way?" inquired the Spirit.

"Remember it!" cried Scrooge with fervor; "I could walk it blindfolded."

"Strange to have forgotten it for so many years!" observed the Ghost. "Let us go on."

They walked along the road, Scrooge recognizing every gate, post, and tree; until a little market town appeared in the distance, with its bridge, its church, its ruined castle, [8] and winding river. Some shaggy ponies now were seen trotting toward them with boys upon their backs, who called to other boys in country gigs and carts, driven by farmers. All these boys were in great spirits and shouted to each other, until the broad fields were so full of merry music that the crisp air laughed to hear it.

"These are but shadows of the things that have been," said the Ghost. "They have no consciousness of us."

The jocund travelers came on; and as they came, Scrooge knew and named them every one. Why was he rejoiced beyond all bounds to see them? Why did his cold eye glisten and his heart leap as they went past? Why was he filled with gladness when he heard them give each other "Merry Christmas" as they parted at crossroads and byways for their several homes? What was "Merry Christmas" to Scrooge? Out upon "Merry Christmas"! What good had it ever done to him?

"The school is not quite deserted," said the Ghost. "A solitary child, neglected by his friends, is left there still."

Scrooge said he knew it. And he sobbed.

They left the highroad by a well-remembered lane and soon approached a mansion [9] of dull red brick, with a little weathercock-surmounted cupola on

---

[8] Hearn reveals that Dickens had included the castle reference in his first manuscript (thus making it evident he was referring to his childhood home: Medway River, Strood, Chatham, and Rochester), but, for some reason, deleted it.

[9] According to Hearn, this was the Wellington Academy where Dickens received a brief year-and-a-half education before leaving at fifteen. A counterpart is in *David Copperfield* as well.

the roof and a bell hanging in it. It was a large house, but one of broken fortunes; for the spacious offices were little used, their walls were damp and mossy, their windows broken, and their gates decayed. Fowls clucked and strutted in the stables; and the coach houses and sheds were overrun with grass. Nor was it more retentive of its ancient state within; for, entering the dreary hall and glancing through the open doors of many rooms, they found them poorly furnished, cold, and vast. There was an earthy savor in the air, a chilly bareness in the place, which associated itself somehow with too much getting up by candlelight and not too much to eat.

They went, the Ghost and Scrooge, across the hall, to a door at the back of the house. It opened before them and disclosed a long, bare, melancholy room, made barer still by lines of plain deal forms[10] and desks. At one of these, a lonely boy was reading[11] near a feeble fire; and Scrooge sat down upon a form and wept to see his poor forgotten self as he used to be.

Not a latent echo in the house, not a squeak and scuffle from the mice behind the paneling, not a drip from the half-thawed waterspout in the dull yard behind, not a sigh among the leafless boughs of one despondent poplar, not the idle swinging of an empty storehouse door, no, not a clicking in the fire, but fell upon the heart of Scrooge with softening influence and gave a freer passage to his tears.

The Spirit touched him on the arm and pointed to his younger self, intent upon his reading. Suddenly, a man in foreign garments, wonderfully real and distinct to look at, stood outside the window, with an ax stuck in his belt and leading by the bridle an ass laden with wood.

"Why, it's Ali Baba!"[12] Scrooge exclaimed in ecstasy. "It's dear old honest Ali Baba! Yes, yes, I know. One Christmastime, when yonder solitary child was left here all alone, he *did* come, for the first time, just like that. Poor boy! And Valentine,"[13] said Scrooge, "and his wild brother, Orson; there they go! And what's his name,[14] who was put down in his drawers, asleep, at the gate of Damascus; don't you see him? And the sultan's groom turned upside down by the genii; there he is upon his head! Serves him right! I'm glad of it. What business had *he* to be married to the princess?"

---

[10] Long, unpainted, unvarnished pine benches.

[11] Dickens, being a sickly boy, more often than not, read while his classmates were playing.

[12] Dickens is now in a childish dreamworld, where figures in the books he read were as real as any he knew outside of books. He loved *The Arabian Nights* as a child.

[13] *The History of the Two Valyannte Brethren* (1495), translated by Henry Watson into English in 1565 (Hearn).

[14] Bedridden Hassan, from *The Arabian Nights*.

To hear Scrooge expending all the earnestness of his nature on such subjects, in a most extraordinary voice between laughing and crying—and to see his heightened and excited face—would have been a surprise to his business friends in the city, indeed.

"There's the parrot!"[15] cried Scrooge. "Green body and yellow tail, with a thing like a lettuce growing out of the top of his head; there he is! 'Poor Robin Crusoe' he called him, when he came home again after sailing around the island. 'Poor Robin Crusoe, where have you been, Robin Crusoe?' The man thought he was dreaming, but he wasn't. It was the parrot, you know. There goes Friday, running for his life to the little creek! Halloa! Hoop! Halloo!"

Then, with a rapidity of transition very foreign to his usual character, he said in pity for his former self, "Poor boy!" and cried again.

"I wish . . . ," Scrooge muttered, putting his hand in his pocket and looking about him after drying his eyes with his cuff. "But it's too late now."

"What is the matter?" asked the Spirit.

"Nothing," said Scrooge. "Nothing. There was a boy singing a Christmas carol at my door last night. I should like to have given him something, that's all."

The Ghost smiled thoughtfully and waved its hand, saying as it did so, "Let us see another Christmas!"

Scrooge's former self grew larger at the words, and the room became a little darker and more dirty. The panels shrank,[16] the windows racked; fragments of plaster fell out of the ceiling, and the naked laths were shown instead. But how all this was brought about, Scrooge knew no more than you do. He only knew that it was quite correct; that everything had happened so; that there he was, alone again, when all the other boys had gone home for the jolly holidays.

He was not reading now, but walking up and down despairingly. Scrooge looked at the Ghost and, with a mournful shaking of his head, glanced anxiously toward the door.

It opened; and a little girl, much younger than the boy, came darting in and, putting her arms about his neck and often kissing him, addressed him as her "dear, dear brother."

"I have come to bring you home, dear brother!" said the child, clapping her tiny hands and bending down to laugh. "To bring you home, home, home!"

"Home, little Fan?"[17] returned the boy.

---

15 From *Robinson Crusoe*, which Dickens read over and over again as a child.

16 A way of expressing the rapid passage of time.

17 Dickens also had a sister named Fanny, who, two years older than he, would die at the age of thirty-eight (see Dickens biography in the introduction), five years after *A Christmas Carol* was written.

"Yes!" said the child, brimful of glee. "Home for good and all. Home for ever and ever. Father is so much kinder than he used to be, that home's like heaven! He spoke so gently to me one dear night when I was going to bed that I was not afraid to ask him once more if you might come home; and he said, yes, you should, and sent me in a coach to bring you. And you're to be a man," said the child, opening her eyes, "and are never to come back here! But first we're to be together all the Christmas long and have the merriest time in all the world."

"You are quite a woman, little Fan!" exclaimed the boy.

She clapped her hands and laughed, and tried to touch his head; but, being too little, laughed again and stood on tiptoe to embrace him. Then she began to drag him, in her childish eagerness, toward the door; and he, nothing loath to go, accompanied her.

A terrible voice in the hall cried, "Bring down Master Scrooge's box, there!" and in the hall appeared the schoolmaster[18] himself, who glared on Master Scrooge with a ferocious condescension and threw him into a dreadful state of mind by shaking hands with him. He then conveyed him and his sister into the veriest old well of a shivering best parlor that ever was seen, where the maps upon the walls and the celestial and terrestrial globes in the windows, were waxy with cold. Here he produced a decanter of curiously light wine[19] and a block of curiously heavy cake, and administered installments of those dainties to the young people. At the same time, he sent out a meager servant to offer a glass of "something" to the postboy,[20] who answered that he thanked the gentleman, but if it was the same tap as he had tasted before, he had rather not. Master Scrooge's trunk being by this time tied onto the top of the chaise,[21] the children bade the schoolmaster good-bye right willingly and, getting into it, drove gaily down the garden sweep,[22] the quick wheels dashing the hoar-frost and snow from off the dark leaves of the evergreens like spray.

"Always a delicate creature, whom a breath might have withered," said the Ghost. "But she had a large heart!"

"So she had," cried Scrooge. "You're right. I will not gainsay it, Spirit. God forbid!"

---

[18] Dickens, like most schoolchildren of his day, experienced very little kindness in school. Many of the schoolmasters were, in fact, sadistic.

[19] Hearn, referencing *Punch*, notes that it was customary at English boarding schools for masters to offer "half-baked cake and home-made wine" to departing students.

[20] Driver of the carriage.

[21] Carriage drawn by one horse.

[22] Curve of the driveway through the grounds.

"She died a woman," said the Ghost, "and had, as I think—"

"One child," Scrooge returned.

"True," said the Ghost. "Your nephew! And she died giving him life; just as, I believe, your mother died giving you life." [23]

Scrooge seemed uneasy in his mind and answered briefly, "Yes."

Although they had but that moment left the school behind them, they were now in the busy thoroughfares of a city, where shadowy passengers passed and repassed; where shadowy carts and coaches battled for the way, and where all the strife and tumult of a real city were. It was made plain enough, by the dressing of the shops, that here, too, it was Christmastime again; but it was evening, and the streets were lighted up.

The Ghost stopped at a certain warehouse door and asked Scrooge if he knew it.

"Know it!" said Scrooge. "Wasn't I apprenticed here?"

They went in. At the sight of an old gentleman in a Welsh wig, sitting behind such a high desk that if he had been two inches taller, he must have knocked his head against the ceiling, Scrooge cried in great excitement, "Why, it's old Fezziwig! Bless his heart, it's Fezziwig alive again!"

Old Fezziwig laid down his pen and looked up at the clock, which pointed to the hour of seven. [24] He rubbed his hands; adjusted his capacious waistcoat; laughed all over himself, from his shoes to his organ of benevolence,[25] and called out in a comfortable, oily, rich, fat, jovial voice, "Yo ho, there! Ebenezer! Dick!"

Scrooge's former self, now grown a young man, came briskly in, accompanied by his fellow apprentice.

"Dick Wilkins, to be sure!" said Scrooge to the Ghost. "Bless me, yes. There he is. He was very much attached to me, was Dick. Poor Dick! Dear, dear!"

"Yo ho, my boys!" said Fezziwig. "No more work tonight. Christmas Eve, Dick. Christmas, Ebenezer! Let's have the shutters up," cried old Fezziwig with a sharp clap of his hands, "before a man can say Jack Robinson!" [26]

You wouldn't believe how those two fellows went at it! They charged into the street with the shutters—one, two, three—had 'em up in their places—four,

---

[23] Apparently, Dickens, in his public readings, may have implied that both women died young, in childbirth—or shortly after—and since that time, in stage, photoplay, and film portrayals of the story, it has occasionally been incorporated into the text.

[24] Businesses were usually open until 9:00 P.M.

[25] Phrenologists, dividing the brain into forty parts, positioned "benevolence" in the forehead, according to Hearn.

[26] Hearn notes that the name came from a seventeenth-century comic song, based on a real person who'd arrive at friends' homes and leave before he could even be announced.

five, six—barred 'em and pinned 'em—seven, eight, nine—and came back before you could have got to twelve, panting like racehorses.

"Hilli-ho!" cried old Fezziwig, skipping down from the high desk with wonderful agility. "Clear away, my lads, and let's have lots of room here! Hilli-ho, Dick! Chirrup, Ebenezer!"

Clear away! There was nothing they wouldn't have cleared away, or couldn't have cleared away, with old Fezziwig looking on. It was done in a minute. Every movable thing was packed off, as if it were dismissed from public life for evermore; the floor was swept and watered, the lamps were trimmed, fuel was heaped upon the fire; and the warehouse was as snug, and warm, and dry, and bright a ballroom as you would desire to see upon a winter's night.

In came a fiddler with a music book; he went up to the lofty desk, made an orchestra of it, and tuned like fifty stomachaches. In came Mrs. Fezziwig, one vast substantial smile. In came the three Miss Fezziwigs, beaming and lovable. In came the six young followers whose hearts they broke. In came all the young men and women employed in the business. In came the housemaid, with her cousin the baker. In came the cook with her brother's particular friend the milkman. In came the boy from over the way, who was suspected of not having board enough from his master; he tried to hide himself behind the girl from next door but one, who was proved to have had her ears pulled by her mistress. In they all came, one after another; some shyly, some boldly, some gracefully, some awkwardly, some pushing, some pulling; in they all came, anyhow and everyhow. Away they all went, twenty couples at once; hands half around and back again the other way; down the middle and up again; round and round in various stages of affectionate grouping; old top couple always turning up in the wrong place; new top couple starting off again, as soon as they got there; all top couples at last, and not a bottom one to help them! When this result was brought about, old Fezziwig, clapping his hands to stop the dance, cried out, "Well done!" and the fiddler plunged his hot face into a pot of porter,[27] especially provided for that purpose. But, scorning rest upon his reappearance, he instantly began again, though there were no dancers yet, as if the other fiddler had been carried home, exhausted, on a shutter; and he were a brand-new man resolved to beat him out of sight or perish.

There were more dances, and there were forfeits,[28] and more dances, and there was cake, and there was negus,[29] and there was a great piece of Cold

[27] A cheap popular ale.

[28] By the early nineteenth century, forfeit payment was usually taken in kisses rather than in coins.

[29] A drink made of wine, hot water, sugar, nutmeg, and lemon juice.

Roast, and there was a great piece of Cold Boiled, and there were mince pies, and plenty of beer. But the great effect of the evening came after the Roast and Boiled, when the fiddler (an artful dog, mind!—the sort of man who knew his business better than you or I could have told it him!) struck up "Sir Roger de Coverley."[30] Then old Fezziwig stood out to dance with Mrs. Fezziwig. Top couple, too; with a good stiff piece of work cut out for them; three- or four-and-twenty pairs of partners; people who were not to be trifled with; people who *would* dance and had no notion of walking.

But if they had been twice as many—ah! four times—old Fezziwig would have been a match for them, and so would Mrs. Fezziwig. As to *her,* she was worthy to be his partner in every sense of the term. If that's not high praise, tell me higher, and I'll use it. A positive light appeared to issue from Fezziwig's calves. They shone in every part of the dance like moons. You couldn't have predicted, at any given time, what would become of them next. And when old Fezziwig and Mrs. Fezziwig had gone all through the dance— advance and retire, hold hands with your partner, bow and curtsy, corkscrew, thread-the-needle, and back again to your place—Fezziwig "cut,"[31] and cut so deftly that he appeared to wink with his legs, and came upon his feet again without a stagger.

When the clock struck eleven, this domestic ball broke up. Mr. and Mrs. Fezziwig took their stations, one on either side the door, and, shaking hands with every person individually as he or she went out, wished him or her a merry Christmas. When everybody had retired but the two apprentices, they did the same to them; and thus the cheerful voices died away, and the lads were left to their beds, which were under a counter in the back shop.

During the whole of this time, Scrooge had acted like a man out of his wits. His heart and soul were in the scene and with his former self. He corroborated everything, remembered everything, enjoyed everything, and underwent the strangest agitation. It was not until now, when the bright faces of his former self and Dick were turned from them, that he remembered the Ghost and became conscious that it was looking full upon him, while the light upon its head burnt very clear.

"A small matter," said the Ghost, "to make these silly folks so full of gratitude."

---

30 Hearn notes that this very popular country dance (dating back to the Normans) was incredibly complicated, only the best dancers being able to do it without a misstep. For good reason, it was generally the last dance of the evening. Dickens himself loved to dance the "Sir Roger de Coverley."

31 A fancy dance step in which a dancer, leaping into the air, alternates his feet (one in front of the other) before touching ground.

"Small!" echoed Scrooge.

The Spirit signed to him to listen to the two apprentices, who were pouring out their hearts in praise of Fezziwig; and when he had done so, it said:

"Why! Is it not? He has spent but a few pounds of your mortal money: three or four, perhaps. Is that so much that he deserves this praise?"

"It isn't that," said Scrooge, heated by the remark and speaking unconsciously like his former, not his latter, self. "It isn't that, Spirit. He has the power to render us happy or unhappy; to make our service light or burdensome; a pleasure or a toil. Say that his power lies in words and looks; in things so slight and insignificant that it is impossible to add and count 'em up. What then? The happiness he gives is quite as great as if it cost a fortune."

He felt the Spirit's glance and stopped.

"What is the matter?" asked the Ghost.

"Nothing particular," said Scrooge.

"Something, I think?" the Ghost insisted.

"No," said Scrooge. "No. I should like to be able to say a word or two to my clerk just now. That's all."

His former self turned down the lamps as he gave utterance to the wish; and Scrooge and the Ghost again stood side by side in the open air.

"My time grows short," observed the Spirit. "Quick!"

This was not addressed to Scrooge, or to anyone whom he could see, but it produced an immediate effect. For again Scrooge saw himself. He was older now; a man in the prime of life. His face had not the harsh and rigid lines of later years; but it had begun to wear the signs of care and avarice. There was an eager, greedy, restless motion in the eye, which showed the passion that had taken root and where the shadow of the growing tree would fall.

He was not alone, but sat by the side of a fair young girl in a mourning dress, in whose eyes there were tears, which sparkled in the light that shone out of the Ghost of Christmas Past.

"It matters little," she said softly. "To you, very little. Another idol has displaced me; and, if it can cheer and comfort you in time to come as I would have tried to do, I have no just cause to grieve."

"What idol has displaced you?" he rejoined.

"A golden one." [32]

"This is the even-handed dealing of the world!" he said. "There is nothing on which it is so hard as poverty; and there is nothing it professes to

---

[32] See Exodus 32.

condemn with such severity as the pursuit of wealth!"

"You fear the world too much," she answered gently. "All your other hopes have merged into the hope of being beyond the chance of its sordid reproach. I have seen your nobler aspirations fall off one by one until the master passion, Gain, engrosses you. Have I not?"

"What then?" he retorted. "Even if I have grown so much wiser, what then? I am not changed toward you."

She shook her head.

"Am I?"

"Our contract is an old one. It was made when we were both poor and content to be so, until, in good season, we could improve our worldly fortune by our patient industry. You are changed. When it was made, you were another man."

"I was a boy," he said impatiently.

"Your own feeling tells you that you were not what you now are," she returned. "I am. That which promised happiness when we were one in heart is fraught with misery now that we are two. How often and how keenly I have thought of this, I will not say. It is enough that I *have* thought of it and can release you from our engagement."[33]

"Have I ever sought release?"

"In words, no. Never."

"In what, then?"

"In a changed nature; in an altered spirit; in another atmosphere of life; another hope as its great end. In everything that made my love of any worth or value in your sight. If this had never been between us," said the girl, looking mildly, but with steadiness, upon him, "tell me, would you seek me out and try to win me now? Ah, no!"

He seemed to yield to the justice of this supposition in spite of himself. But he said, with a struggle, "You think not."

"I would gladly think otherwise if I could," she answered. "Heaven knows! When *I* have learned a truth like this, I know how strong and irresistible it must be. But if you were free today, tomorrow, yesterday, can even I believe that you would choose a dowerless girl[34] —you who, in your absolute confidence in her, weigh everything by Gain; or, choosing her, if for a moment you were false enough to your one guiding principle to do so, do I not know

---

33 Hearn notes that in his later public readings, to make it clear to audiences what the agreement was, Dickens added the word "engagement."

34 Apparently, her parents have recently died, leaving her nothing for a dowry.

that your repentance and regret would surely follow? I do—and I release you. With a full heart, for the love of him you once were."

He was about to speak; but, with her head turned from him, she resumed:

"You may—the memory of what is past half makes me hope you will—have pain in this. A very, very brief time, and you will dismiss the recollection of it gladly, as an unprofitable dream, from which it happened well that you awoke. May you be happy in the life you have chosen!"

She left him, and they parted.

"Spirit," said Scrooge, "show me no more! Conduct me home. Why do you delight to torture me?"

"One shadow more!" exclaimed the Ghost.

"No more!" cried Scrooge. "No more! I don't wish to see it. Show me no more!"

But the relentless ghost pinioned him in both its arms and forced him to observe what happened next.

They were in another scene and place—a room, not very large or handsome, but full of comfort. Near to the winter fire sat a beautiful young girl, so like that last that Scrooge believed it was the same, until he saw *her*, now a comely matron, sitting opposite her daughter. The noise in this room was perfectly tumultuous, for there were more children there than Scrooge in his agitated state of mind could count; and, unlike the celebrated herd in the poem,[35] they were not forty children conducting themselves like one, but every child was conducting itself like forty. The consequences were uproarious beyond belief; but no one seemed to care; on the contrary, the mother and daughter laughed heartily and enjoyed it very much; and the latter, soon beginning to mingle in the sports, got pillaged by the young brigands most ruthlessly.

What would I not have given to be one of them! Though I never could have been so rude, no, no! I wouldn't for the wealth of all the world have crushed that braided hair and torn it down; and for the precious little shoe, I wouldn't have plucked it off, God bless my soul, to save my life! As to measuring her waist in sport, as they did—bold young brood—I couldn't have done it; I should have expected my arm to have grown around it for a punishment and never come straight again. And yet I should have dearly liked, I own, to have touched her lips, to have questioned her, that she might have opened them; to have looked upon the lashes of her downcast eyes and never raised a blush; to have let loose waves of hair, an inch of which would be a keepsake beyond price—in short, I should have liked, I do confess, to

---

[35] "Written in March" (1802), by William Wordsworth.

have had the lightest license of a child and yet to have been man enough to know its value.

But now a knocking at the door was heard, and such a rush immediately ensued that she, with laughing face and plundered dress, was borne toward it in the center of a flushed and boisterous group, just in time to greet the father, who came home attended by a man laden with Christmas toys and presents. Then the shouting and the struggling, and the onslaught that was made on the defenseless porter! The scaling him, with chairs for ladders, to dive into his pockets, despoil him of brown-paper parcels, hold on tight by his cravat, hug him around his neck, pummel his back, and kick his legs in irrepressible affection! The shouts of wonder and delight with which the discovery of every package was received! The terrible announcement that the baby had been taken in the act of putting a doll's frying pan into his mouth and was more than suspected of having swallowed a fictitious turkey glued on a wooden platter! The immense relief of finding this a false alarm! The joy, and gratitude, and ecstasy! They are all indescribable alike. It is enough that, by degrees, the children and their emotions got out of the parlor and, by one stair at a time, up to the top of the house; where they went to bed and so subsided.

And now Scrooge looked on more attentively than ever, when the master of the house, having his daughter leaning fondly on him, sat down with her and her mother at his own fireside—and when he thought that such another creature, quite as graceful and as full of promise, might have called him Father and been a springtime in the haggard winter of his life, his sight grew very dim indeed.

"Belle," said the husband, turning to his wife with a smile, "I saw an old friend of yours this afternoon."

"Who was it?"

"Guess!"

"How can I? Tut, don't I know?" she added in the same breath, laughing as he laughed. "Mr. Scrooge."

"Mr. Scrooge it was. I passed his office window; and as it was not shut up and he had a candle inside, I could scarcely help seeing him. His partner lies upon the point of death, I hear; and there he sat alone. Quite alone in the world, I do believe."

"Spirit!" said Scrooge in a broken voice. "Remove me from this place."

"I told you these were shadows of the things that have been," said the Ghost. "That they are what they are do not blame me!"

"Remove me!" Scrooge exclaimed, "I cannot bear it!"

The Extinguisher

He turned upon the Ghost and, seeing that it looked upon him with a face, in which in some strange way there were fragments of all the faces it had shown him, wrestled with it.

"Leave me! Take me back. Haunt me no longer!"

In the struggle, if that can be called a struggle in which the Ghost with no visible resistance on its own part was undisturbed by any effort of its adversary, Scrooge observed that its light was burning high and bright; and dimly connecting that with its influence over him, he seized the extinguisher cap and, by a sudden action, pressed it down upon its head.

The Spirit dropped beneath it, so that the extinguisher covered its whole form; but though Scrooge pressed it down with all his force, he could not hide the light,[36] which streamed from under it, in an unbroken flood upon the ground.

He was conscious of being exhausted and overcome by an irresistible drowsiness; and, further, of being in his own bedroom. He gave the cap a parting squeeze, in which his hand relaxed; and had barely time to reel to bed, before he sank into a heavy sleep.

---

36 Hearn feels the significance here is that, try as he may, Scrooge cannot snuff out—or forget—the lessons the Spirit has taught him. And this First Spirit, essentially a radiant effervescent candle, is a symbol for memory, which can be fully extinguished only by death.

THE SECOND OF THE THREE SPIRITS

A waking in the middle of a prodigiously tough snore, and sitting up in bed to get his thoughts together, Scrooge had no occasion to be told that the bell was again upon the stroke of one. He felt that he was restored to consciousness in the right nick of time, for the special purpose of holding a conference with the second messenger dispatched to him through Jacob Marley's intervention. But finding that he turned uncomfortably cold when he began to wonder which of his curtains this new specter would draw back, he put them every one aside with his own hands and, lying down again, established a sharp lookout all around the bed. For he wished to challenge the Spirit on the moment of its appearance and did not wish to be taken by surprise and made nervous.

Gentlemen of the free-and-easy[1] sort, who plume themselves on being acquainted with a move or two,[2] and being usually equal to the time of day,[3] express the wide range of their capacity for adventure by observing that they are good for anything from pitch-and-toss to manslaughter; between which opposite extremes, no doubt, there lies a tolerably wide and comprehensive range of subjects. Without venturing for Scrooge quite as hardily as this, I

---

[1] Sporting type—someone who likes to smoke, drink, roister, gamble.

[2] Worldly.

[3] Ready for whatever happens.

43

Scrooge's Third Visitor

don't mind calling on you to believe that he was ready for a good broad field of strange appearances, and that nothing between a baby and a rhinoceros would have astonished him very much.

Now, being prepared for almost anything, he was not by any means prepared for nothing; and consequently, when the bell struck one, and no shape appeared, he was taken with a violent fit of trembling. Five minutes, ten minutes, a quarter of an hour went by, yet nothing came. All this time he lay upon his bed, the very core and center of a blaze of ruddy light, which streamed upon it when the clock proclaimed the hour; and which, being only light, was more alarming than a dozen ghosts, as he was powerless to make out what it meant, or would be at; and was sometimes apprehensive that he might be at that very moment an interesting case of spontaneous combustion, without having the consolation of knowing it. At last, however, he began to think—as you or I would have thought at first; for it is always the person not in the predicament who knows what ought to have been done in it and would unquestionably have done it, too—at last, I say, he began to think that the source and secret of this ghostly light might be in the adjoining room: from whence, on further tracing it, it seemed to shine. This idea taking full possession of his mind, he got up softly and shuffled in his slippers to the door.

The moment Scrooge's hand was on the lock, a strange voice called him by his name and bade him enter. He obeyed.

It was his own room. There was no doubt about that. But it had undergone a surprising transformation. The walls and ceiling were so hung with living green,[4] that it looked a perfect grove; from every part of which bright gleaming berries glistened. The crisp leaves of holly, mistletoe, and ivy reflected back the light, as if so many little mirrors had been scattered there; and such a mighty blaze went roaring up the chimney as that dull petrification of a hearth had never known in Scrooge's time, or Marley's, or for many and many a winter season gone. Heaped up on the floor, to form a kind of throne, were turkeys, geese, game, poultry, brawn,[5] great joints of meat, sucking pigs,[6] long wreaths of sausages, mince pies, plum puddings, barrels of oysters, red-hot chestnuts, cherry-cheeked apples, juicy oranges, luscious pears, immense twelfth-cakes,[7] and seething bowls of

---

[4] Evergreens.

[5] Boar flesh.

[6] Not more than four weeks old (often roasted whole).

[7] A large pastry frosted and highly decorated (usually served on Twelfth Night/Epiphany). Inside is a bean or coin, and whoever bites down on the prize becomes king or queen of the celebration.

punch,[8] that made the chamber dim with their delicious steam. In easy state upon this couch there sat a jolly Giant,[9] glorious to see, who bore a glowing torch, in shape not unlike Plenty's horn,[10] and held it up, high up, to shed its light on Scrooge as he came peeping around the door.

"Come in!" exclaimed the Ghost. "Come in and know me better, man!"

Scrooge entered timidly and hung his head before this Spirit. He was not the dogged Scrooge he had been; and though the Spirit's eyes were clear and kind, he did not like to meet them.

"I am the Ghost of Christmas Present," said the Spirit. "Look upon me!"

Scrooge reverently did so. It was clothed in one simple deep-green robe, or mantle, bordered with white fur. This garment hung so loosely on the figure, that its capacious breast[11] was bare, as if disdaining to be warded or concealed by any artifice. Its feet, observable beneath the ample folds of the garment, were also bare; and on its head it wore no other covering than a holly wreath, set here and there with shining icicles. Its dark-brown curls were long and free; free as its genial face, its sparkling eyes, its open hand, its cheery voice, its unconstrained demeanor, and its joyful air. Girded around its middle was an antique scabbard; but no sword was in it, and the ancient sheath was eaten up with rust.[12]

"You have never seen the like of me before!" exclaimed the Spirit.

"Never," Scrooge made answer to it.

"Have never walked forth with the younger members of my family; meaning (for I am very young) my elder brothers born in these later years?" pursued the Phantom.

"I don't think I have," said Scrooge. "I am afraid I have not. Have you had many brothers, Spirit?"

"More than eighteen hundred,"[13] said the Ghost.

"A tremendous family to provide for," muttered Scrooge.

The Ghost of Christmas Present rose.

"Spirit," said Scrooge submissively, "conduct me where you will. I went forth last night on compulsion, and I learned a lesson that is working now.

---

[8] Probably wassail.

[9] Similar to Father Christmas.

[10] Cornucopia.

[11] Traditionally, the center of emotion.

[12] Father Christmas is often depicted in armor. Dickens suggests by the empty scabbard and rust that Christ and Christian goodwill conquer all.

[13] To be exact: 1,842.

Tonight if you have aught to teach me, let me profit by it."

"Touch my robe!"

Scrooge did as he was told and held it fast.

Holly, mistletoe, red berries, ivy, turkeys, geese, game, poultry, brawn, meat, pigs, sausages, oysters, pies, puddings, fruit, and punch, all vanished instantly. So did the room, the fire, the ruddy glow, the hour of night; and they stood in the city streets on Christmas morning, where (for the weather was severe) the people made a rough, but brisk and not unpleasant kind of music in scraping the snow from the pavement in front of their dwellings and from the tops of their houses: whence it was mad delight to the boys to see it come plumping down into the road below and splitting into artificial little snowstorms.

The house fronts looked black enough, and the windows blacker, contrasting with the smooth white sheet of snow upon the roofs, and with the dirtier snow upon the ground; which last deposit had been plowed up in deep furrows by the heavy wheels of the carts and wagons: furrows that crossed and recrossed each other hundreds of times where the great streets branched off, and they made intricate channels, hard to trace in the thick yellow mud and icy water. The sky was gloomy, and the shortest streets were choked up with a dingy mist, half-thawed, half-frozen, whose heavier particles descended in a shower of sooty atoms, as if all the chimneys in Great Britain had, by one consent, caught fire and were blazing away to their dear hearts' content. There was nothing very cheerful in the climate or the town, and yet there was an air of cheerfulness abroad that the clearest summer air and brightest summer sun might have endeavored to diffuse in vain.

For the people who were shoveling away on the housetops were jovial and full of glee; calling out to one another from the parapets and now and then exchanging a facetious snowball—better-natured missile far than many a wordy jest—laughing heartily if it went right, and not less heartily if it went wrong. The poulterers' shops were still half-open, and the fruiterers' were radiant in their glory. There were great, round, potbellied baskets of chestnuts, shaped like the waistcoats of jolly old gentlemen, lolling at the doors, and tumbling out into the street in their apoplectic opulence. There were ruddy, brown-faced, broad-girthed Spanish onions, shining in the fatness of their growth like Spanish friars, and winking from their shelves in wanton slyness at the girls as they went by and glanced demurely at the hung-up mistletoe. There were pears and apples clustered high in blooming pyramids; there were bunches of grapes, made, in the shopkeepers' benevolence, to dangle from conspicuous hooks that people's mouths might water gratis as they passed; there were piles of filberts, mossy and brown, recalling, in their fragrance, ancient walks among the woods and pleasant shufflings ankle deep through withered leaves; there were Norfolk Biffins,[14] squab and swarthy, setting off the yellow of the oranges and lemons, and, in the great compactness of their juicy persons, urgently entreating and beseeching to be carried home in paper bags and eaten after dinner.

The very gold and silver fish,[15] set forth among these choice fruits in a bowl, though members of a dull and stagnant-blooded race, appeared to know that there was something going on; and, to a fish, went gasping round and round their little world in slow and passionless excitement.

The grocers'! Oh, the grocers'—nearly closed, with perhaps two shutters down, or one; but through those gaps such glimpses! It was not alone that the scales descending on the counter made a merry sound, or that the twine and roller parted company so briskly, or that the canisters were rattled up and down like juggling tricks, or even that the blended scents of tea and coffee were so grateful to the nose, or even that the raisins were so plentiful and rare, the almonds so extremely white, the sticks of cinnamon so long and straight, the other spices so delicious, the candied fruits so caked and spotted with molten sugar as to make the coldest lookers-on feel faint and subsequently bilious. Nor was it that the figs were moist and pulpy, or that the French plums blushed in modest tartness from their highly decorated boxes, or that everything was good to eat and in its Christmas dress. But the customers were all so hurried and so eager in the hopeful promise of the day that they tumbled up against each other at the door, crashing their wicker baskets wildly, and left their purchases upon the counter, and came running back to fetch them, and committed hundreds of the like mistakes, in the best humor possible; while the grocer and his people were so frank and eager that the polished hearts with which they fastened their aprons behind might have been their own, worn outside for general inspection and for Christmas daws to peck at if they chose.[16]

But soon the steeples called good people all, to church and chapel, and away they came, flocking through the streets in their best clothes and with their merriest faces. And at the same time there emerged, from scores of bystreets,

---

[14] A cooking apple with a red-rust skin.

[15] Carp.

[16] A tradition dating back to medieval times—wearing one's heart on a sleeve—but it also meant "for folks to find fault with" (according to Hearn).

lanes, and nameless turnings, innumerable people, carrying their dinners to the bakers' shops. The sight of these poor revelers appeared to interest the Spirit very much, for it stood with Scrooge beside it in a baker's doorway and, taking off the covers as their bearers passed, sprinkled incense[17] on their dinners from his torch. And it was a very uncommon kind of torch, for once or twice, when there were angry words between some dinner-carriers who had jostled each other, he shed a few drops of water on them from it, and their good humor was restored directly. For they said it was a shame to quarrel upon Christmas Day. And so it was! God love it, so it was!

In time the bells ceased, and the bakers were shut up; and yet there was a genial shadowing forth of all these dinners, and the progress of their cooking, in the thawed blotch of wet above each baker's oven, where the pavement smoked as if its stones were cooking, too.

"Is there a peculiar flavor in what you sprinkle from your torch?" asked Scrooge.

"There is. My own."

"Would it apply to any kind of dinner on this day?" asked Scrooge.

"To any kindly given. To a poor one most."

"Why to a poor one most?" asked Scrooge.

"Because it needs it most."

"Spirit!" said Scrooge after a moment's thought. "I wonder you, of all the beings in the many worlds about us, should desire to cramp these people's opportunities of innocent enjoyment."

"I!" cried the Spirit.

"You would deprive them of their means of dining every seventh day, often the only day on which they can be said to dine at all," said Scrooge. "Wouldn't you?"

"I!" cried the Spirit.

"You seek to close these places on the Seventh Day,"[18] said Scrooge. "And it comes to the same thing."

"I seek!" exclaimed the Spirit.

"Forgive me if I am wrong. It has been done in your name, or at least in that of your family," said Scrooge.

"There are some upon this earth of yours," returned the Spirit, "who lay claim to know us, and who do their deeds of passion, pride, ill will, hatred, envy, bigotry, and selfishness in our name, who are as strange to us, and all

---

17 One of the gifts of the Magi to the Christ Child.

18 Sir Andrew Agnew tried a number of times in the 1830s to institute a Sunday Blue Law, closing bakeries and other places where food was available.

our kith and kin, as if they had never lived. Remember that, and charge their doings on themselves, not us."

Scrooge promised that he would; and they went on, invisible, as they had been before, into the suburbs of the town. It was a remarkable quality of the Ghost (which Scrooge had observed at the baker's) that, notwithstanding its gigantic size, it could accommodate itself to any place with ease; and that it stood beneath a low roof quite as gracefully and like a supernatural creature as it was possible it could have done in any lofty hall.

And perhaps it was the pleasure the good Spirit had in showing off this power, or else it was its own kind, generous, hearty nature, and its sympathy with all poor men, that led it straight to Scrooge's clerk's; for there it went, and took Scrooge with it, holding on to its robe; and on the threshold of the door, the Spirit smiled and stopped to bless Bob Cratchit's [19] dwelling with the sprinklings of its torch. Think of that! Bob had but fifteen "bob" [20] a week himself; he pocketed on Saturdays but fifteen copies of his Christian name; and yet the Ghost of Christmas Present blessed his four-roomed house! [21]

Then up rose Mrs. Cratchit, Cratchit's wife, dressed out but poorly in a twice-turned gown, but brave in ribbons, which are cheap and make a goodly show for sixpence; and she laid the cloth, assisted by Belinda Cratchit, second of her daughters, also brave in ribbons; while Master Peter Cratchit plunged a fork into the saucepan of potatoes, and getting the corners of his monstrous shirt collar (Bob's private property, conferred upon his son and heir in honor of the day) into his mouth, rejoiced to find himself so gallantly attired and yearned to show his linen in the fashionable Parks. And now two smaller Cratchits, boy and girl, came tearing in, screaming that outside the baker's they had smelled the goose and known it for their own; and basking in luxurious thoughts of sage and onion, these young Cratchits danced about the table and exalted Master Peter Cratchit to the skies, while he (not proud, although his collars nearly choked him) blew the fire, until the slow potatoes, bubbling up, knocked loudly at the saucepan lid to be let out and peeled.

"What has ever got your precious father, then?" said Mrs. Cratchit. "And

[19] Hearn points out that "cratch" is an old English word for "crèche"; but his name also suggests the scratching quill pens in those days.

[20] A Cockney word for a shilling (12 pence); taken from "baubee," a debased Scottish coin. Hearn (referencing C. Z. Barnett) notes that Cratchit's Christmas dinner (seven shillings for the goose, five for the pudding, three for the onions, sage, and oranges) represented nearly a full week's wages for him.

[21] Dickens lived in a similar four-room house as a child in Camden Town. Hearn notes that the six Cratchit children correspond in age and sex to the six in Dickens's family: Fanny, Charles, Letitia, Frederick, Harriet, and Alfred (Martha, Peter, Belinda, boy, girl, Tiny Tim).

your brother Tiny Tim?[22] And Martha wasn't as late last Christmas Day by half an hour!"

"Here's Martha, Mother!" said a girl, appearing as she spoke.

"Here's Martha, Mother!" cried the two young Cratchits. "Hurrah! There's such a goose, Martha!"

"Why, bless your heart alive, my dear, how late you are!" said Mrs. Cratchit, kissing her a dozen times and taking off her shawl and bonnet for her with officious zeal.

"We'd a deal of work to finish up last night," replied the girl, "and had to clear away this morning, Mother!"

"Well! Never mind so long as you are come," said Mrs. Cratchit. "Sit ye down before the fire, my dear, and have a warm,[23] Lord bless ye!"

"No, no! There's Father coming," cried the two young Cratchits, who were everywhere at once. "Hide, Martha, hide!"

So Martha hid herself, and in came little Bob, the father, with at least three feet of scarf, exclusive of the fringe, hanging down before him, and his threadbare clothes darned up and brushed, to look seasonable, and Tiny Tim upon his shoulder. Alas for Tiny Tim! He bore a little crutch and had his legs supported by an iron frame.

"Why, where's our Martha?" cried Bob Cratchit, looking around.

"Not coming," said Mrs. Cratchit.

"Not coming!" said Bob with a sudden declension in his high spirits; for he had been Tim's racehorse all the way from church and had come home rampant. "Not coming on Christmas Day!"

Martha didn't like to see him disappointed, even if it were only in joke; so she came out prematurely from behind the closet door and ran into his arms, while the two young Cratchits hustled Tiny Tim and bore him off into the washhouse, that he might hear the pudding singing in the copper.[24]

"And how did little Tim behave?" asked Mrs. Cratchit when she had rallied Bob on his credulity, and Bob had hugged his daughter to his heart's content.

"As good as gold," said Bob, "and better. Somehow, he gets thoughtful, sitting by himself so much, and thinks the strangest things you ever heard. He

---

22 Earlier to be named "Little Fred" after Dickens's brother Alfred. In October 1843, while visiting his sister Fan and her invalid son, Harry Burnett, in Manchester, Dickens found the inspiration for Tiny Tim. Later, Hearn reminds us, when the boy died young, Dickens used him again as the lost boy: Paul Dombey.

23 A state of gradually warming up.

24 A boiler (used for washing clothes).

told me, coming home, that he hoped the people saw him in the church,[25] because he was a cripple, and it might be pleasant to them to remember upon Christmas Day who made lame beggars walk and blind men see."[26]

Bob's voice was tremulous when he told them this, and it trembled more when he said that Tiny Tim was growing strong and hearty.

His active little crutch was heard upon the floor, and back came Tiny Tim before another word was spoken, escorted by his brother and sister to his stool beside the fire; and while Bob, turning up his cuffs—as if, poor fellow, they were capable of being made more shabby—compounded some hot mixture in a jug with gin and lemons, stirred it round and round, and put it on the hob to simmer, Master Peter and the two ubiquitous young Cratchits went to fetch the goose, with which they soon returned in high procession.

Such a bustle ensued that you might have thought a goose the rarest of all birds; a feathered phenomenon, to which a black swan was a matter of course—and, in truth, it was something very like it in that house. Mrs. Cratchit made the gravy (ready beforehand in a little saucepan) hissing hot; Master Peter mashed the potatoes with incredible vigor; Miss Belinda sweetened up the applesauce; Martha dusted the hot plates; Bob took Tiny Tim beside him in a tiny corner at the table; the two young Cratchits set chairs for everybody, not forgetting themselves, and, mounting guard upon their posts, crammed spoons into their mouths, lest they should shriek for goose before their turn came to be helped.

At last the dishes were set on, and grace was said. It was succeeded by a breathless pause, as Mrs. Cratchit, looking slowly all along the carving knife, prepared to plunge it in the breast; but when she did, and when the long-expected gush of stuffing issued forth, one murmur of delight arose all around the board, and even Tiny Tim, excited by the two young Cratchits, beat on the table with the handle of his knife and feebly cried, "Hurrah!"

There never was such a goose. Bob said he didn't believe there ever was such a goose cooked. Its tenderness and flavor, size and cheapness, were the themes of universal admiration. Eked out by applesauce and mashed potatoes, it was a sufficient dinner for the whole family; indeed, as Mrs. Cratchit said with great delight (surveying one small atom of a bone upon the dish), they hadn't even eaten it all! Yet everyone had had enough, and the youngest Cratchits, in particular, were steeped in sage and onion to the eyebrows! But

---

[25] St. Stephen's Church in Camden Town.

[26] John 5, Mark 8.

now, the plates being changed by Miss Belinda, Mrs. Cratchit left the room alone—too nervous to bear witnesses—to take the pudding up and bring it in.

Suppose it should not be done enough! Suppose it should break in turning out! Suppose somebody should have got over the wall of the backyard and stolen it,[27] while they were merry with the goose—a supposition at which the two young Cratchits became livid! All sorts of horrors were supposed.

Hallo! A great deal of steam! The pudding was out of the copper. A smell like a washing day! That was the cloth. A smell like an eating-house, and a pastry cook's next door to each other, with a laundress's next door to that! That was the pudding! In half a minute, Mrs. Cratchit entered—flushed, but smiling proudly—with the pudding, like a speckled cannonball, so hard and firm, blazing in half of half-a-quartern[28] of ignited brandy, and bedight[29] with Christmas holly stuck into the top.

Oh, a wonderful pudding! Bob Cratchit said—and calmly, too—that he regarded it as the greatest success achieved by Mrs. Cratchit since their marriage. Mrs. Cratchit said that, now that the weight was off her mind, she would confess she had had her doubts about the quantity of flour. Everybody had something to say about it, but nobody said or thought it was at all a small pudding for a large family. It would have been flat heresy to do so. Any Cratchit would have blushed to hint at such a thing.

At last the dinner was all done, the cloth was cleared, the hearth swept, and the fire made up. The compound in the jug being tasted and considered perfect, apples and oranges were put upon the table and a shovel full of chestnuts on the fire. Then all the Cratchit family drew around the hearth in what Bob Cratchit called a circle, meaning half a one; and at Bob Cratchit's elbow stood the family display of glass: two tumblers and a custard cup without a handle.

These held the hot stuff from the jug, however, as well as golden goblets would have done; and Bob served it out with beaming looks, while the chestnuts on the fire sputtered and cracked noisily. Then Bob proposed:

"A merry Christmas to us all, my dears. God bless us!"

Which all the family reechoed.

"God bless us, every one!" said Tiny Tim, the last of all.

---

27 This all too frequently happened in that district.

28 One quarter of a pint.

29 Adorned; dressed.

He sat very close to his father's side, upon his little stool. Bob held his withered little hand in his, as if he loved the child and wished to keep him by his side, and dreaded that he might be taken from him.

"Spirit," said Scrooge with an interest he had never felt before, "tell me if Tiny Tim will live."[30]

"I see a vacant seat," replied the Ghost, "in the poor chimney corner, and a crutch without an owner, carefully preserved. If these shadows remain unaltered by the future, the child will die."

"No, no," said Scrooge. "Oh, no, kind Spirit! Say he will be spared."

"If these shadows remain unaltered by the future, none other of my race," returned the Ghost, "will find him here. What then? If he be like to die, he had better do it and decrease the surplus population."

Scrooge hung his head to hear his own words quoted by the Spirit and was overcome with penitence and grief.

"Man," said the Ghost, "if man you be in heart, not adamant, forbear that wicked cant until you have discovered what the surplus is, and where it is. Will you decide what men shall live, what men shall die? It may be that, in the sight of heaven, you are more worthless and less fit to live than millions like this poor man's child. O God! To hear the insect on the leaf pronouncing on the too much life among his hungry brothers in the dust!"

Scrooge bent before the Ghost's rebuke and, trembling, cast his eyes upon the ground. But he raised them speedily on hearing his own name.

"Mr. Scrooge!" said Bob. "I'll give you Mr. Scrooge, the founder of the feast!"

"The founder of the feast, indeed!" cried Mrs. Cratchit, reddening. "I wish I had him here. I'd give him a piece of my mind to feast upon, and I hope he'd have a good appetite for it."

"My dear," said Bob, "the children! Christmas Day."

"It should be Christmas Day, I am sure," said she, "on which one drinks the health of such an odious, stingy, hard, unfeeling man as Mr. Scrooge. You know he is, Robert! Nobody knows it better than you do, poor fellow!"

"My dear!" was Bob's mild answer. "Christmas Day."

"I'll drink his health for your sake and the day's," said Mrs. Cratchit, "not for his. Long life to him! A merry Christmas and a happy New Year! He'll be very merry and very happy, I have no doubt!"

---

[30] Hearn notes that this exchange was not in the original manuscript; however, Dickens, while reading his galleys, felt it important to offer some hope for Tiny Tim's survival, so he added these lines.

The children drank the toast after her. It was the first of their proceedings that had no heartiness in it. Tiny Tim drank it last of all, but he didn't care two-pence for it. Scrooge was the ogre of the family. The mention of his name cast a dark shadow on the party, which was not dispelled for a full five minutes.

After it had passed away, they were ten times merrier than before, from the mere relief of Scrooge the Baleful being done with. Bob Cratchit told them how he had a situation in mind for Master Peter, which would bring in, if obtained, full five-and-sixpence weekly. The two young Cratchits laughed tremendously at the idea of Peter's being a man of business; and Peter himself looked thoughtfully at the fire from between his collars, as if he were delib-erating what particular investments he should favor when he came into the receipt of that bewildering income. Martha, who was a poor apprentice at a milliner's, then told them what kind of work she had to do, and how many hours she worked at a stretch, and how she meant to lie abed tomorrow morning for a good long rest; tomorrow being a holiday she passed at home. Also how she had seen a countess and a lord some days before, and how the lord "was much about as tall as Peter"; at which Peter pulled up his collar so high that you couldn't have seen his head if you had been there. All this time the chestnuts and the jug went round and round; and by and by they had a song, about a lost child traveling in the snow, from Tiny Tim, who had a plaintive little voice and sang it very well indeed.

There was nothing of high mark in this. They were not a handsome family; they were not well dressed; their shoes were far from being water-proof; their clothes were scanty; and Peter might have known, and very likely did, the inside of a pawnbroker's.[31] But they were happy, grateful, pleased with one another, and contented with the time; and when they faded, and looked happier yet in the bright sprinklings of the Spirit's torch at parting, Scrooge had his eye upon them, and especially on Tiny Tim, until the last.

By this time, it was getting dark and snowing pretty heavily; and as Scrooge and the Spirit went along the streets, the brightness of the roaring fires in kitchens, parlors, and all sorts of rooms was wonderful. Here, the flickering of the blaze showed preparations for a cozy dinner, with hot plates baking through and through before the fire, and deep-red curtains, ready to be drawn to shut out cold and darkness. There, all the children of the house were running out into the snow to meet their married sisters, brothers, cousins, uncles, and aunts, and be the first to greet them. Here, again, were

---

31 As a child, Dickens was invariably the one sent to pawn family goods in order to have enough food in the house to eat.

shadows on the window blinds of guests assembling; and there a group of handsome girls, all hooded and fur-booted, and all chattering at once, tripped lightly off to some near neighbor's house; where, woe upon the single man who saw them enter—artful witches, well they knew it—in a glow!

But if you had judged from the numbers of people on their way to friendly gatherings, you might have thought that no one was at home to give them welcome when they got there, instead of every house expecting company and piling up its fires half-chimney high. Blessings on it, how the Ghost exulted! How it bared its breadth of breast, and opened its capacious palm, and floated on, outpouring with a generous hand its bright and harmless mirth on everything within its reach! The very lamplighter, who ran on before, dotting the dusky street with specks of light, and who was dressed to spend the evening somewhere, laughed out loudly as the Spirit passed, though little knew the lamplighter that he had any company but Christmas.

And now, without a word of warning from the Ghost, they stood upon a bleak and desert moor, where monstrous masses of rude stone were cast about, as though it were the burial place of giants;[32] and water spread itself wheresoever it listed—or would have done so, but for the frost that held it prisoner; and nothing grew but moss and furze,[33] and coarse, rank grass. Down in the west, the setting sun had left a streak of fiery red, which glared upon the desolation for an instant, like a sullen eye, and frowning lower, lower, lower yet, was lost in the thick gloom of darkest night.

"What place is this?" asked Scrooge.

"A place where miners live,[34] who labor in the bowels of the earth," returned the Spirit. "But they know me. See!"

A light shone from the window of a hut, and swiftly they advanced toward it. Passing through the wall of mud and stone, they found a cheerful company assembled around a glowing fire. An old, old man and woman, with their children and their children's children, and another generation beyond that, were all decked out gaily in their holiday attire. The old man, in a voice that seldom rose above the howling of the wind upon the barren waste, was singing them a Christmas song; it had been a very old song when he was a boy; and from time to time, they all joined in the chorus. So surely

---

[32] Setting: the coast of Cornwall, the traditional setting for the "Jack the Giant Killer" story.

[33] Gorse.

[34] Land's End, Cornwall—most likely, the Botallick Mine.

as they raised their voices, the old man got quite blithe and loud; and so surely as they stopped, his vigor sank again.

The Spirit did not tarry here, but bade Scrooge hold its robe and, passing on above the moor, sped whither? Not to sea? To sea. To Scrooge's horror, looking back, he saw the last of the land, a frightful range of rocks, behind them; and his ears were deafened by the thundering of water, as it rolled, and roared, and raged among the dreadful caverns it had worn as it fiercely tried to undermine the earth.

Built upon a dismal reef of sunken rocks, some league or so from shore, on which the waters chafed and dashed the wild year through, there stood a solitary lighthouse. [35] Great heaps of seaweed clung to its base, and stormbirds—born of the wind, one might suppose, as seaweed of the water—rose and fell about it, like the waves they skimmed.

But, even here, two men who watched the light had made a fire that through the loophole in the thick stone wall shed out a ray of brightness on the awful sea. Joining their horny hands over the rough table at which they sat, they wished each other "Merry Christmas" in their can of grog; and one of them—the elder, too, with his face all damaged and scarred with hard weather, as the figurehead of an old ship might be—struck up a sturdy song that was like a gale in itself.

Again the Ghost sped on, above the black and heaving sea—on, on—until being far away, as it told Scrooge, from any shore, they alighted on a ship. They stood beside the helmsman at the wheel, the lookout in the bow, the officers who had the watch; dark, ghostly figures in their several stations; but every man among them hummed a Christmas tune, or had a Christmas thought, or spoke below his breath to his companion of some bygone Christmas Day, with homeward hopes belonging to it. And every man on board, waking or sleeping, good or bad, had had a kinder word for one another on that day than on any day in the year; and had shared to some extent in its festivities; and had remembered those he cared for at a distance, and had known that they delighted to remember him.

It was a great surprise to Scrooge, while listening to the moaning of the wind and thinking what a solemn thing it was to move on through the lonely darkness over an unknown abyss, whose depths were secrets as profound as death—it was a great surprise to Scrooge, while thus engaged, to hear a hearty laugh. It was a much greater surprise to Scrooge to recognize it as his own

---

35 Probably Longships Lighthouse.

nephew's and to find himself in a bright, dry, gleaming room, with the Spirit stand-ing smiling by his side and looking at that same nephew with approving affability!

"Ha, ha!" laughed Scrooge's nephew. "Ha, ha, ha!"

If you should happen, by any unlikely chance, to know a man more blessed in a laugh than Scrooge's nephew, all I can say is, I should like to know him, too. Introduce him to me, and I'll cultivate his acquaintance.

It is a fair, evenhanded, noble adjustment of things that while there is infec-tion in disease and sorrow, there is nothing in the world so irresistibly contagious as laughter and good humor. When Scrooge's nephew laughed in this way—holding his sides, rolling his head, and twisting his face into the most extravagant contortions—Scrooge's niece, by marriage, laughed as heartily as he. And their assembled friends, being not a bit behindhand, roared out lustily.

"Ha, ha! Ha, ha, ha, ha!"

"He said that Christmas was a humbug, as I live!" cried Scrooge's nephew. "He believed it, too!"

"More shame for him, Fred!" said Scrooge's niece indignantly. Bless those women! They never do anything by halves. They are always in earnest.

She was very pretty—exceedingly pretty. With a dimpled, surprised-looking, capital face; a ripe little mouth that seemed made to be kissed—as no doubt it was; all kinds of good little dots about her chin that melted into one another when she laughed; and the sunniest pair of eyes you ever saw in any little crea-ture's head. Altogether she was what you would have called provoking,[36] you know; but satisfactory, too. Oh, perfectly satisfactory!

"He's a comical old fellow," said Scrooge's nephew, "that's the truth; and not so pleasant as he might be. However, his offenses carry their own punishment, and I have nothing to say against him."

"I'm sure he is very rich, Fred," hinted Scrooge's niece. "At least, you always tell me so."

"What of that, my dear?" said Scrooge's nephew. "His wealth is of no use to him. He doesn't do any good with it. He doesn't make himself comfortable with it. He hasn't the satisfaction of thinking—ha, ha, ha!—that he is ever going to benefit us with it."

"I have no patience with him," observed Scrooge's niece. Scrooge's niece's sisters, and all the other ladies, expressed the same opinion.

"Oh, I have!" said Scrooge's nephew. "I am sorry for him; I couldn't be angry with him if I tried. Who suffers by his ill whims? Himself always. Here he takes it into his head to dislike us, and he won't come and dine with us.

---

36 Provocative.

What's the consequence? He doesn't lose much of a dinner."

"Indeed, I think he loses a very good dinner," interrupted Scrooge's niece. Everybody else said the same, and they must be allowed to have been competent judges, because they had just had dinner; and with the dessert upon the table, they were clustered around the fire, by lamplight.

"Well! I am very glad to hear it," said Scrooge's nephew, "because I haven't any great faith in these young housekeepers. What do *you* say, Topper?"

Topper had clearly got his eye upon one of Scrooge's niece's sisters, for he answered that a bachelor was a wretched outcast, who had no right to express an opinion on the subject. Whereat Scrooge's niece's sister—the plump one with the lace tucker, not the one with the roses—blushed.

"Do go on, Fred," said Scrooge's niece, clapping her hands. "He never finishes what he begins to say! He is such a ridiculous fellow!"

Scrooge's nephew reveled in another laugh, and as it was impossible to keep the infection off, though the plump sister tried hard to do it with aromatic vinegar, his example was unanimously followed.

"I was only going to say," said Scrooge's nephew, "that the consequence of his taking a dislike to us, and not making merry with us, is, as I think, that he loses some pleasant moments, which could do him no harm. I am sure he loses pleasanter companions than he can find in his own thoughts, either in his moldy old office or his dusty chambers. I mean to give him the same chance every year, whether he likes it or not, for I pity him. He may rail at Christmas till he dies, but he can't help thinking better of it—I defy him— if he finds me going there, in good temper, year after year, and saying, 'Uncle Scrooge, how are you?' If it only puts him in the vein to leave his poor clerk fifty pounds, *that's* something; and I think I shook him yesterday."

It was their turn to laugh now, at the notion of his shaking Scrooge. But being thoroughly good-natured, and not much caring what they laughed at, so that they laughed at any rate, he encouraged them in their merriment and passed the bottle joyously.

After tea they had some music. For they were a musical family and knew what they were about when they sang a Glee[37] or Catch,[38] I can assure you—especially Topper, who could growl away in the bass like a good one and never swell the large veins in his forehead or get red in the face over it. Scrooge's niece played well upon the harp; and she played, among other

---

[37] A musical composition for three or more voices (usually light or secular).

[38] A comic canon (or round) for three or more voices (each singing a different line simultaneously).

tunes, a simple little air (a mere nothing—you might learn to whistle it in two minutes) that had been familiar to the child who fetched Scrooge from the boarding school, as he had been reminded by the Ghost of Christmas Past. When this strain of music sounded, all the things that the Ghost had shown him came upon his mind; he softened more and more and thought that if he could have listened to it often, years ago, he might have cultivated the kindnesses of life for his own happiness with his own hands, without resorting to the sexton's spade that buried Jacob Marley.

But they didn't devote the whole evening to music. After a while, they played at forfeits; for it is good to be children sometimes, and never better than at Christmas, when its mighty Founder was a child Himself. Stop! There was first a game at blindman's buff. Of course there was. And I no more believe Topper was really blind than I believe he had eyes in his boots. My opinion is that it was a done thing between him and Scrooge's nephew; and that the Ghost of Christmas Present knew it. The way he went after that plump sister in the lace tucker was an outrage on the credulity of human nature. Knocking down the fire irons, tumbling over the chairs, bumping up against the piano, smothering himself among the curtains, wherever she went, there went he! He always knew where the plump sister was. He wouldn't catch anybody else. If you had fallen up against him on purpose (as some of them did), he would have made a feint of endeavoring to seize you, which would have been an affront to your understanding, and would instantly have sidled off in the direction of the plump sister. She often cried out that it wasn't fair; and it really was not. But when, at last, he caught her; when, in spite of all her silken rustlings and her rapid flutterings past him, he got her into a corner whence there was no escape, then his conduct was the most execrable. For his pretending not to know her—his pretending that it was necessary to touch her headdress, and further to assure himself of her identity by pressing a certain ring upon her finger and a certain chain about her neck—was vile, monstrous! No doubt she told him her opinion of it when, another blind man being in office, they were so very confidential together behind the curtains.

Scrooge's niece was not one of the blindman's buff party, but was made comfortable with a large chair and a footstool, in a snug corner where the Ghost and Scrooge were close behind her. But she joined in the forfeits and loved her love to admiration with all the letters of the alphabet.[39] Likewise at

---

[39] A parlor game: "I love my love with an A," each player having to complete sentences with each letter of the alphabet. The game was also used to teach children the alphabet.

the game of How, When, and Where,[40] she was very great and, to the secret joy of Scrooge's nephew, beat her sisters hollow; though they were sharp girls, too, as Topper could have told you. There might have been twenty people there, young and old, but they all played, and so did Scrooge; for wholly forgetting, in the interest he had in what was going on, that his voice made no sound in their ears, he sometimes came out with his guess quite loud and very often guessed right, too; for the sharpest needle, best Whitechapel,[41] warranted not to cut in the eye, was not sharper than Scrooge, blunt as he took it in his head to be.

The Ghost was greatly pleased to find him in this mood, and it looked upon him with such favor that he begged like a boy to be allowed to stay until the guests departed. But this the Spirit said could not be done.

"Here is a new game," said Scrooge. "One half hour, Spirit, only one!"

It was a game called Yes and No,[42] where Scrooge's nephew had to think of something, and the rest must find out what, he only answering to their questions yes or no, as the case was. The brisk fire of questioning to which he was exposed elicited from him that he was thinking of an animal, a live animal, rather a disagreeable animal, a savage animal, an animal that growled and grunted sometimes, and talked sometimes and lived in London, and walked about the streets, and wasn't made a show of, and wasn't led by anybody, and didn't live in a menagerie, and was never killed in a market, and was not a horse, or an ass, or a cow, or a bull, or a tiger, or a dog, or a pig, or a cat, or a bear. At every fresh question that was put to him, this nephew burst into a fresh roar of laughter and was so inexpressibly tickled that he was obliged to get up off the sofa and stamp. At last the plump sister, falling into a similar state, cried out:

"I have found it out! I know what it is, Fred! I know what it is!"

"What is it?" cried Fred.

"It's your uncle Scro-o-o-oge."

Which it certainly was. Admiration was the universal sentiment, though some objected that the reply to "Is it a bear?" ought to have been "Yes"; inasmuch as an answer in the negative was sufficient to have diverted their thoughts from Mr. Scrooge, supposing they had ever had any tendency that way.

---

40 A game of forfeits, in which each player in turn must ask, "How do you like it?" "When do you like it?" "Where do you like it?"

41 A London district known for making needles.

42 Dickens loved this game.

"He has given us plenty of merriment, I am sure," said Fred, "and it would be ungrateful not to drink his health. Here is a glass of mulled wine ready to our hand at the moment; and I say, 'Uncle Scrooge!'"

"Well! Uncle Scrooge!" they cried.

"A merry Christmas and a happy New Year to the old man, whatever he is!" said Scrooge's nephew. "He wouldn't take it from me, but may he have it, nevertheless. Uncle Scrooge!"

Uncle Scrooge had imperceptibly become so happy and light of heart that he would have pledged the unconscious company in return, and thanked them in an inaudible speech, if the Ghost had given him time. But the whole scene passed off in the breath of the last word spoken by his nephew—and he and the Spirit were again upon their travels.

Much they saw, and far they went, and many homes they visited, but always with a happy end. The Spirit stood beside sickbeds, and they were cheerful; on foreign lands, and they were close at home; by struggling men, and they were patient in their greater hope; by poverty, and it was rich. In almshouse, hospital, and jail, in misery's every refuge, where vain man in his little brief authority had not made fast the door and barred the Spirit out, it left its blessing and taught Scrooge its precepts.

It was a long night, if it were only a night; but Scrooge had his doubts of this, because the Christmas holidays appeared to be condensed into the space of time they passed together. It was strange, too, that, while Scrooge remained unaltered in his outward form, the Ghost grew older, clearly older. Scrooge had observed this change, but never spoke of it until they left a children's Twelfth-Night party,[43] when, looking at the Spirit as they stood together in an open place, he noticed that its hair was gray.

"Are spirits' lives so short?" asked Scrooge.

"My life upon this globe is very brief," replied the Ghost. "It ends tonight."

"Tonight!" cried Scrooge.

"Tonight at midnight. Hark! The time is drawing near."

The chimes were ringing three-quarters past eleven at that moment.

"Forgive me if I am not justified in what I ask," said Scrooge, looking intently at the Spirit's robe, "but I see something strange and not belonging to yourself, protruding from your skirts. Is it a foot or a claw?"

---

[43] In Dickens's time, the Christmas season lasted until Epiphany. The Dickens family always loved the Twelfth Night parties their father put on for them.

Ignorance and Want

"It might be a claw, for the flesh there is upon it," was the Spirit's sorrowful reply. "Look here!"

From the foldings of its robe it brought two children, wretched, abject, frightful, hideous, miserable. They knelt down at its feet and clung to the outside of its garment.

"O man! Look here! Look, look down here!" exclaimed the Ghost.

They were a boy and girl. Yellow, meager, ragged, scowling, wolfish, but prostrate, too, in their humility. Where graceful youth should have filled their features out and touched them with its freshest tints, a stale and shriveled hand, like that of age, had pinched and twisted them and pulled them into shreds. Where angels might have sat enthroned, devils lurked and glared out menacingly. No change, no degradation, no perversion of humanity in any grade, through all the mysteries of wonderful creation, has monsters half so horrible and dreadful.

Scrooge started back, appalled. Having them shown to him in this way, he tried to say they were fine children, but the words choked themselves, rather than be parties to a lie of such enormous magnitude.

"Spirit, are they yours?" Scrooge could say no more.

"They are man's," said the Spirit, looking down upon them. "And they cling to me, appealing from their fathers. This boy is Ignorance. This girl is Want. [44] Beware of them both, and all of their degree, but most of all beware of this boy, for on his brow I see that written which is Doom, unless the writing be erased. Deny it!" cried the Spirit, stretching out his hand toward the city. "Slander those who tell it ye! Admit it for your factious purposes, and make it worse! And bide the end!"

"Have they no refuge or resource?" cried Scrooge.

"Are there no prisons?" said the Spirit, turning on him for the last time with his own words. "Are there no workhouses?"

The bell struck twelve. [45]

Scrooge looked about him for the Ghost and saw it not. As the last stroke ceased to vibrate, he remembered the prediction of old Jacob Marley and,

---

[44] Through these two children, Dickens hoped readers of the story would commit themselves to making a difference in the lives of poor children. His inspiration came from the terrible schools for poor—or "ragged"—children, and so many more were in slums, mines, chimneys (see William Blake's "The Chimney Sweeper"), and prisons.

[45] The hour corresponds to the Twelfth Day of Christmas. Hearn notes that while the first two Ghosts appeared at one (the beginning of day), the black-shrouded Ghost appears at twelve, the traditional bewitching hour.

lifting up his eyes, beheld a solemn Phantom, draped and hooded, coming like a mist along the ground toward him.

THE LAST OF THE SPIRITS

The Phantom[1] slowly, gravely, silently approached. When it came near him, Scrooge bent down upon his knee; for in the very air through which this Spirit moved, it seemed to scatter gloom and mystery.

It was shrouded in a deep black garment, which concealed its head, its face, its form, and left nothing of it visible, save one outstretched hand. But for this, it would have been difficult to detach its figure from the night and separate it from the darkness by which it was surrounded.

He felt that it was tall and stately when it came beside him, and that its mysterious presence filled him with a solemn dread. He knew no more, for the Spirit neither spoke nor moved.

"Am I in the presence of the Ghost of Christmas Yet to Come?" asked Scrooge.

The Spirit answered not, but pointed onward with its hand.

"You are about to show me shadows of the things that have not happened, but will happen in the time before us," Scrooge pursued. "Is that so, Spirit?"

The upper portion of the garment was contracted for an instant in its folds, as if the Spirit had inclined its head. That was the only answer he received.

---

[1] The Third Ghost is, of course, Death. Hearn notes that Christmas comes at the end—or death—of a year, and that the birth of Christ is itself a reminder of the crucifixion—as pointed out in the spiritual *I Wonder as I Wander:* "How Jesus the Savior was born for to die."

Although well used to ghostly company by this time, Scrooge feared the silent shape so much that his legs trembled beneath him, and he found that he could hardly stand when he prepared to follow it. The Spirit paused a moment, as observing his condition and giving him time to recover.

But Scrooge was all the worse for this. It thrilled him with a vague, uncertain horror to know that, behind the dusky shroud, there were ghostly eyes intently fixed upon him, while he, though he stretched his own to the utmost, could see nothing but a spectral hand and one great heap of black.

"Ghost of Christmas Yet to Come," he exclaimed, "I fear you more than any specter I have seen. But as I know your purpose is to do me good, and as I hope to live to be another man from what I was, I am prepared to bear your company, and do it with a thankful heart. Will you not speak to me?"

It gave him no reply. The hand was pointed straight before them.

"Lead on!" said Scrooge. "Lead on! The night is waning fast, and it is precious time to me, I know. Lead on, Spirit!"

The Phantom moved away as it had come toward him. Scrooge followed in the shadow of its robe.

They scarcely seemed to enter the city, for the city rather seemed to spring up about them and encompass them of its own act. But there they were in the heart of it; on the Exchange, among the merchants, who hurried up and down, and chinked the money in their pockets, and conversed in groups, and looked at their watches, and trifled thoughtfully with their great gold seals, and so forth, as Scrooge had seen them do often.

The Spirit stopped beside one little knot of businessmen. Observing that the hand was pointed to them, Scrooge advanced to listen to their talk.

"No," said a great fat man with a monstrous chin, "I don't know much about it either way. I only know he's dead."

"When did he die?" inquired another.

"Last night, I believe."

"Why, what was the matter with him?" asked a third, taking a vast quantity of snuff out of a very large snuffbox. "I thought he'd never die."

"God knows," said the first with a yawn.

"What has he done with his money?" asked a red-faced gentleman with a pendulous excrescence[2] on the end of his nose, which shook like the gills of a turkey-cock.

"I haven't heard," said the man with the large chin, yawning again. "Left it to his company, perhaps. He hasn't left it to *me*. That's all I know."

---

2 A hanging wart.

This pleasantry was received with a general laugh.

"It's likely to be a very cheap funeral," said the same speaker, "for, upon my life, I don't know of anybody to go to it. Suppose we make up a party and volunteer?"

"I don't mind going if a lunch is provided," observed the gentleman with the excrescence on his nose. "But I must be fed if I go to one."

Another laugh.

"Well, I am the most disinterested among you, after all," said the first speaker, "for I never wear black gloves,[3] and I never eat lunch. But I'll offer to go if anybody else will. When I come to think of it, I'm not at all sure but that I wasn't his most particular friend,[4] for we used to stop and speak whenever we met. Bye, bye!"

Speakers and listeners strolled away and mixed with other groups. Scrooge knew the men and looked toward the Spirit for an explanation.

The Phantom glided on into a street. Its finger pointed to two persons meeting. Scrooge listened again, thinking that the explanation might lie here.

He knew these men, also, perfectly. They were men of business: very wealthy and of great importance. He had always made a point of standing well in their esteem: in a business point of view, that is; strictly in a business point of view.

"How are you?" said one.

"How are you?" returned the other.

"Well," said the first, "Old Scratch[5] has got his own at last, hey?"

"So I am told," returned the second. "Cold, isn't it?"

"Seasonable for Christmastime. You are not a skater, I suppose?"

"No, no. Something else to think of. Good morning!"

Not another word. That was their meeting, their conversation, and their parting.

Scrooge was at first inclined to be surprised that the Spirit should attach importance to conversations apparently so trivial; but feeling assured that they must have some hidden purpose, he set himself to consider what it was likely to be. They could scarcely be supposed to have any bearing on the death of Jacob, his old partner, for that was past, and this Ghost's province was the future. Nor could he think of anyone immediately connected with

---

3 Given to those who attended English funerals.

4 Hearn points out what an insult this represents from a supposed friend: not to attend the funeral even when bribed to do so by a set of gloves and a free meal.

5 The devil.

himself to whom he could apply them. But not doubting that, to whomsoever they applied, they had some latent moral for his own improvement, he resolved to treasure up every word he heard and everything he saw; and especially to observe the shadow of himself when it appeared. For he had an expectation that the conduct of his future self would give him the clue he missed and would render the solution of these riddles easy.

He looked about in that very place for his own image, but another man stood in his accustomed corner; and though the clock pointed to his usual time of day for being there, he saw no likeness of himself among the multitudes that poured in through the Porch. It gave him little surprise, however; for he had been revolving in his mind a change of life and thought and hoped he saw his newborn resolutions carried out in this.

Quiet and dark beside him stood the Phantom, with its outstretched hand. When he roused himself from his thoughtful quest, he fancied, from the turn of the hand and its position in reference to himself, that the unseen eyes were looking at him keenly. It made him shudder and feel very cold.

They left the busy scene and went into an obscure part of the town, where Scrooge had never penetrated before, although he recognized its situation and its bad repute. The ways were foul and narrow; the shops and houses wretched; the people half-naked, drunken, slipshod, ugly. Alleys and archways, like so many cesspools, disgorged their offenses of smell and dirt and life upon the straggling streets; and the whole quarter reeked with crime, with filth, with misery.

Far into this den of infamous resort, there was a low-browed, beetling[6] shop, below a penthouse roof,[7] where iron, old rags, bottles, bones, and greasy offal were bought. Upon the floor within were piled up heaps of rusty keys, nails, chains, hinges, files, scales, weights, and refuse iron of all kinds. Secrets that few would like to scrutinize were bred and hidden in mountains of unseemly rags, masses of corrupted fat,[8] and sepulchers of bones. Sitting in among the wares he dealt in, by a charcoal stove made of old bricks, was a gray-haired rascal, nearly seventy years of age, who had screened himself from the cold air without by a frowsy curtaining of miscellaneous tatters hung upon a line. There he smoked his pipe in all the luxury of calm retirement.

Scrooge and the Phantom came into the presence of this man just as a

---

[6] Projecting; overhanging.

[7] A roof sloping up a wall.

[8] Grease, drippings, and kitchen waste were purchased and resold: the grease for candles and soap, the drippings as a butter substitute.

woman with a heavy bundle slunk into the shop. But she had scarcely entered, when another woman, similarly laden, came in, too; and she was closely followed by a man in faded black, who was no less startled by the sight of them than they had been upon the recognition of each other. After a short period of blank astonishment, in which the old man with the pipe had joined them, they all three burst into a laugh.

"Let the charwoman[9] alone to be the first!" cried she who had entered first. "Let the laundress alone to be the second; and let the undertaker's man alone to be the third. Look here, Old Joe, here's a chance! If we haven't all three[10] met here without meaning it!"

"You couldn't have met in a better place," said Old Joe, removing his pipe from his mouth. "Come into the parlor. You were made free of it long ago, you know; and the other two ain't strangers. Stop till I shut the door of the shop. Ah! How it shrieks! There ain't such a rusty bit of metal in the place as its own hinges, I believe; and I'm sure there's no such old bones here as mine. Ha! Ha! We're all suitable to our calling, we're well matched. Come into the parlor. Come into the parlor."

The parlor was the space behind the screen of rags. The old man raked the fire together with an old stair-rod[11] and, having trimmed his smoky lamp (for it was night) with the stem of his pipe, put it into his mouth again.

While he did this, the woman who had already spoken threw her bundle on the floor and sat down in a flaunting manner on a stool, crossing her elbows on her knees and looking with a bold defiance at the other two.

"What odds,[12] then? What odds, Mrs. Dilber?" said the woman. "Every person has a right to take care of themselves. *He* always did!"

"That's true, indeed!" said the laundress. "No man more so."

"Why, then, don't stand staring as if you was afraid, woman! Who's the wiser? We're not going to pick holes in each other's coats,[13] I suppose?"

"No indeed!" said Mrs. Dilber and the man together. "We should hope not."

"Very well then!" cried the woman. "That's enough. Who's the worse for the loss of a few things like these? Not a dead man, I suppose?"

---

9 A temporary servant (hired by the day) to do odd housework. This one most likely was hired by the person who was settling the estate.

10 Reminiscent of the three ghoulish witches in *Macbeth*.

11 A brass bar that keeps stair carpets down.

12 Means "What does it matter?"

13 Means "to have a quarrel."

"No indeed," said Mrs. Dilber, laughing.

"If he wanted to keep 'em after he was dead, a wicked old miser," pursued the woman, "why wasn't he natural in his lifetime? If he had been, he'd have had somebody to look after him when he was struck by Death, instead of lying gasping out his last there, alone by himself."

"It's the truest word that ever was spoke," said Mrs. Dilber. "It's a judgment on him."

"I wish it was a little heavier judgment," replied the woman. "It should have been, you may depend upon it, if I could have laid my hands on anything else. Open that bundle, Old Joe, and let me know the value of it. Speak out plain. I'm not afraid to be the first, nor afraid for them to see it. We know pretty well that we were helping ourselves before we met here, I believe. It's no sin. Open the bundle, Joe."

But the gallantry of her friends would not allow this; and the man in faded black, mounting the breach [14] first, produced *his* plunder. It was not extensive. A seal or two, a pencil case, a pair of sleeve buttons, and a brooch of no great value [15] were all. They were severally examined and appraised by Old Joe, who chalked the sums he was disposed to give for each upon the wall and added them up into a total when he found that there was nothing more to come.

"That's your account," said Joe, "and I wouldn't give another sixpence, if I was to be boiled for not doing it. Who's next?"

Mrs. Dilber was next. Sheets and towels, a little wearing apparel, two old-fashioned silver teaspoons, a pair of sugar tongs, and a few boots. Her account was stated on the wall in the same manner.

"I always give too much to ladies. It's a weakness of mine, and that's the way I ruin myself," said Old Joe. "That's your account. If you asked me for another penny and made it an open question, I'd repent of being so liberal and knock off half-a-crown."

"And now undo *my* bundle, Joe," said the first woman.

Joe went down on his knees for the greater convenience of opening it and, having unfastened a great many knots, dragged out a large, heavy roll of some dark stuff.

"What do you call this?" said Joe. "Bed curtains!"

"Ah!" returned the woman, laughing and leaning forward on her crossed arms. "Bed curtains!"

"You don't mean to say you took 'em down, rings and all, with him lying

---

14 Means "taking the lead."

15 Found by this undertaker's assistant on the body or in the clothes he put on the body.

there?" said Joe.

"Yes, I do," replied the woman. "Why not?"

"You were born to make your fortune," said Joe, "and you'll certainly do it."

"I certainly shan't hold back my hand, when I can get anything in it by reaching it out, for the sake of such a man as he was, I promise you, Joe," returned the woman coolly. "Don't drop that oil upon the blankets, now."

"His blankets?" asked Joe.

"Whose else's do you think?" replied the woman. "He isn't likely to take cold without 'em, I dare say."

"I hope he didn't die of anything catching! Eh?" said Old Joe, stopping in his work and looking up.

"Don't you be afraid of that," returned the woman. "I ain't so fond of his company that I'd loiter about him for such things, if he did. Ah! You may look through that shirt till your eyes ache, but you won't find a hole in it, nor a threadbare place. It's the best he had, and a fine one, too. They'd have wasted it, if it hadn't been for me."

"What do you call wasting of it?" asked Old Joe.

"Putting it on him to be buried in, to be sure," replied the woman with a laugh. "Somebody was fool enough to do it, but I took it off again. If calico ain't good enough for such a purpose, it isn't good enough for anything. It's quite as becoming to the body. He can't look uglier than he did in that one."

Scrooge listened to this dialogue in horror. As they sat grouped about their spoil, in the scanty light afforded by the old man's lamp, he viewed them with a detestation and disgust that could hardly have been greater, though they had been obscene demons marketing the corpse itself.

"Ha, ha!" laughed the same woman when Old Joe produced a flannel bag with money in it and doled out their several gains upon the ground. "This is the end of it, you see! He frightened everyone away from him when he was alive, to profit us when he was dead! Ha, ha, ha!"

"Spirit!" said Scrooge, shuddering from head to foot. "I see, I see. The case of this unhappy man might be my own. My life tends that way now. Merciful heaven, what is this?"

He recoiled in terror, for the scene had changed and now he almost touched a bed—a bare, uncurtained bed—on which, beneath a ragged sheet, there lay a something covered up, which, though it was mute, announced itself in awful language.

The room was very dark, too dark to be observed with any accuracy, though Scrooge glanced around it in obedience to a secret impulse, anxious to know what kind of room it was. A pale light, rising in the outer air, fell straight upon the bed; and on it, plundered and bereft, unwatched, unwept over, uncared for—was the body of this man.

Scrooge glanced toward the Phantom. Its steady hand was pointed to the head. The cover was so carelessly adjusted that the slightest raising of it, the motion of a finger upon Scrooge's part, would have disclosed the face. He thought of it, felt how easy it would be to do, and longed to do it; but he had no more power to withdraw the veil than to dismiss the specter at his side.

Oh, cold, cold, rigid, dreadful Death, set up thine altar here, and dress it with such terrors as thou hast at thy command; for this is thy dominion! But of the loved, revered, and honored head thou canst not turn one hair to thy dread purposes, or make one feature odious. It is not that the hand is heavy and will fall down when released; it is not that the heart and pulse are still; but that the hand was open, generous, and true; the heart brave, warm, and tender, and the pulse a man's. Strike, Shadow, strike! And see his good deeds springing from the wound, to sow the world with his life immortal!

No voice pronounced these words in Scrooge's ears, and yet he heard them when he looked upon the bed. He thought, if this man could be raised up now, what would be his foremost thoughts? Avarice, hard dealing, griping cares? They have brought him to a rich end, truly!

He lay in the dark, empty house, with not a man, a woman, or a child to say he was kind to me in this or that, and for the memory of one kind word I will be kind to him. A cat was tearing at the door, and there was a sound of gnawing rats beneath the hearthstone. What *they* wanted in the room of death, and why they were so restless and disturbed, Scrooge did not dare to think.

"Spirit," he said, "this is a fearful place. In leaving it, I shall not leave its lesson, trust me. Let us go!"

Still the Ghost pointed with an unmoved finger to the head.

"I understand you," Scrooge returned, "and I would do it if I could. But I have not the power, Spirit. I have not the power."

Again it seemed to look upon him.

"If there is any person in the town who feels emotion caused by this man's death," said Scrooge, quite agonized, "show that person to me, Spirit, I beseech you!"

The Phantom spread its dark robe before him for a moment, like a wing, and, withdrawing it, revealed a room by daylight, where a mother and her children were.

She was expecting someone, and with anxious eagerness; for she walked up and down the room, started at every sound, looked out from the window,

The Last of the Spirits

glanced at the clock, tried but in vain to work with her needle, and could hardly bear the voices of her children in their play.

At length, the long-expected knock was heard. She hurried to the door and met her husband, a man whose face was careworn and depressed, though he was young. There was a remarkable expression in it now: a kind of serious delight of which he felt ashamed and which he struggled to repress.

He sat down to the dinner that she had been hoarding for him by the fire, and when she asked him faintly what news (which was not until after a long silence), he appeared embarrassed how to answer.

To help him, she asked, "Is it good, or bad?"

"Bad," he answered.

"We are quite ruined?"

"No. There is hope yet, Caroline."

"If *he* relents," she said, amazed, "there is! Nothing is past hope, if such a miracle has happened."

"He is past relenting," said her husband. "He is dead."

She was a mild and patient creature, if her face spoke truth; but she was thankful in her soul to hear it, and she said so with clasped hands. She prayed forgiveness the next moment, and was sorry; but the first was the emotion of her heart.

"What the half-drunken woman, whom I told you of last night, said to me when I tried to see him and obtain a week's delay—and what I thought was a mere excuse to avoid me—turns out to have been quite true. He was not only very ill, but dying, then."

"To whom will our debt be transferred?"

"I don't know. But, before that time, we shall be ready with the money; and even though we were not, it would be bad fortune indeed to find so merciless a creditor in his successor. We may sleep tonight with light hearts, Caroline!"

Yes. Soften it as they would, their hearts were lighter. The children's faces, hushed and clustered around to hear what they so little understood, were brighter; and it was a happier house for this man's death! The only emotion that the Ghost could show him, caused by the event, was one of pleasure.

"Let me see some tenderness connected with a death," said Scrooge, "or that dark chamber, Spirit, that we left just now will be forever present to me."

The Ghost conducted him through several streets familiar to his feet; and as they went along, Scrooge looked here and there to find himself, but nowhere was he to be seen. They entered poor Bob Cratchit's house, the dwelling he had visited before, and found the mother and the children seated around the fire.

Quiet. Very quiet. The noisy little Cratchits were as still as statues in one corner and sat looking up at Peter, who had a book before him. The mother and her daughters were engaged in sewing. But surely they were very quiet!

"'And he took a child and set him in the midst of them.'" [16]

Where had Scrooge heard those words? He had not dreamed them. The boy must have read them out as he and the Spirit crossed the threshold. Why did he not go on?

The mother laid her work upon the table and put her hand up to her face.

"The color [17] hurts my eyes," she said.

The color? Ah, poor Tiny Tim!

"They're better now again," said Cratchit's wife. "It makes them weak by candlelight; and I wouldn't show weak eyes to your father when he comes home for the world. It must be near his time."

"Past it rather," Peter answered, shutting up his book. "But I think he has walked a little slower than he used to, these few last evenings, Mother."

They were very quiet again.

At last she said in a steady, cheerful voice that only faltered once, "I have known him walk with—I have known him walk with Tiny Tim upon his shoulder very fast indeed."

"And so have I," cried Peter. "Often."

"And so have I," exclaimed another. So had all.

"But he was very light to carry," she resumed, intent upon her work, "and his father loved him so, that it was no trouble—no trouble. And there is your father at the door!"

She hurried out to meet him; and little Bob in his scarf—he had need of it, poor fellow—came in. His tea was ready for him on the hob, and they all tried to see who should help him to it first. Then the two young Cratchits got upon his knees and laid, each child, a little cheek against his face, as if they said, *Don't mind it, Father. Don't be grieved!*

Bob was very cheerful with them and spoke pleasantly to all the family. He looked at the work upon the table and praised the industry and speed of Mrs. Cratchit and the girls. They would be done long before Sunday, he said.

"Sunday! You went today, then, Robert?" said his wife.

---

[16] One of Dickens's favorite Bible passages (Matthew 18:2, Mark 9:36), and he amplified them in his book *The Life of Our Lord* (1849).

[17] Mrs. Cratchit and the girls are sewing their mourning clothes.

"Yes, my dear," returned Bob. "I wish you could have gone. It would have done you good to see how green a place it is. But you'll see it often. I promised him that I would walk there on a Sunday. My little, little child!" cried Bob. "My little child!"

He broke down all at once. He couldn't help it. If he could have helped it, he and his child would have been further apart, perhaps, than they were.

He left the room and went upstairs into the room above, which was lighted cheerfully and hung with Christmas. There was a chair set close beside the child, and there were signs of someone having been there lately. Poor Bob sat down in it, and when he had thought a little and composed himself, he kissed the little face. He was reconciled to what had happened and went down again quite happy.

They drew about the fire and talked, the girls and mother working still. Bob told them of the extraordinary kindness of Mr. Scrooge's nephew, whom he had scarcely seen but once, and who, meeting him in the street that day and seeing that he looked a little—"just a little down, you know"—inquired what had happened to distress him. "On which," said Bob, "for he is the pleasantest-spoken gentleman you ever heard, I told him. 'I am heartily sorry for it, Mr. Cratchit,' he said, 'and heartily sorry for your good wife.' By-the-by, how he ever knew *that, I* don't know."

"Knew what, my dear?"

"Why, that you were a good wife," replied Bob.

"Everybody knows that," said Peter.

"Very well observed, my boy!" cried Bob. "I hope they do. 'Heartily sorry,' he said, 'for your good wife. If I can be of service to you in any way,' he said, giving me his card, 'that's where I live. Pray come to me.' Now, it wasn't," cried Bob, "for the sake of anything he might be able to do for us, so much as for his kind way, that this was quite delightful. It really seemed as if he had known our Tiny Tim and felt with us."

"I'm sure he's a good soul!" said Mrs. Cratchit.

"You would be surer of it, my dear," returned Bob, "if you saw and spoke to him. I shouldn't be at all surprised—mark what I say!—if he got Peter a better situation."

"Only hear that, Peter," said Mrs. Cratchit.

"And then," cried one of the girls, "Peter will be keeping company with someone[18] and setting up for himself."

"Get along with you!" retorted Peter, grinning.

---

[18] Of marrying age.

"It's just as likely as not," said Bob, "one of these days; though there's plenty of time for that, my dear. But however and whenever we part from one another, I am sure we shall none of us forget poor Tiny Tim, shall we? —or this first parting that there was among us?"

"Never, Father!" they all cried.

"And I know," said Bob, "I know, my dears, that when we recollect how patient and how mild he was; although he was a little, little child, we shall not quarrel easily among ourselves and forget poor Tiny Tim in doing it."

"No, never, Father!" they all cried again.

"I am very happy," said little Bob. "I am very happy!"

Mrs. Cratchit kissed him, his daughters kissed him, the two young Cratchits kissed him, and he shook hands with Peter. Spirit of Tiny Tim, thy childish essence was from God!

"Specter," said Scrooge, "something informs me that our parting moment is at hand. I know it, but I know not how. Tell me what man that was whom we saw lying dead?"

The Ghost of Christmas Yet to Come conveyed him, as before—though at a different time, he thought. Indeed, there seemed to be no order in these latter visions, save that they were in the future—into the resorts of business-men, but showed him not himself. Indeed, the Spirit did not stay for anything, but went straight on, as to the end just now desired, until besought by Scrooge to tarry for a moment.

"This court," said Scrooge, "through which we hurry now is where my place of occupation is, and has been for a length of time. I see the house. Let me behold what I shall be in days to come."

The Spirit stopped; the hand was pointed elsewhere.

"The house is yonder," Scrooge exclaimed. "Why do you point away?"

The inexorable finger underwent no change.

Scrooge hastened to the window of his office and looked in. It was an office still, but not his. The furniture was not the same, and the figure in the chair was not himself. The Phantom pointed as before.

He joined it once again and, wondering why and whither he had gone, accompanied it until they reached an iron gate. He paused to look around before entering.

A churchyard. [19] Here, then, the wretched man, whose name he had now to learn, lay underneath the ground. It was a worthy place. Walled in by

---

[19] All Hallows Staining, Star Alley, off Mark Lane, in the Langborn Ward (Hearn referencing Gwen Major).

houses; overrun by grass and weeds, the growth of vegetation's death,[20] not life; choked up with too much burying; fat with repleted appetite.[21] A worthy place!

The Spirit stood among the graves and pointed down to one. Scrooge advanced toward it, trembling. The Phantom was exactly as it had been, but he dreaded that he saw new meaning in its solemn shape.

"Before I draw nearer to that stone to which you point," said Scrooge, "answer me one question. Are these the shadows of the things that *will* be, or are they shadows of the things that *may* be only?"

Still the Ghost pointed downward to the grave by which it stood.

"Men's courses will foreshadow certain ends, to which, if persevered in, they must lead," said Scrooge. "But if the courses be departed from, the ends will change. Say it is thus with what you show me!"

The Spirit was immovable as ever.

Scrooge crept toward it, trembling as he went; and, following the finger, read upon the stone of the neglected grave his own name: EBENEZER SCROOGE.

"Am *I* that man who lay upon the bed?" he cried upon his knees.

The finger pointed from the grave to him and back again.

"No, Spirit! Oh no, no!"

The finger still was there.

"Spirit," he cried, tightly clutching at its robe, "hear me! I am not the man I was. I will not be the man I must have been but for this intercourse. Why show me this, if I am past all hope?"

For the first time, the hand appeared to shake.

"Good Spirit," he pursued as down upon the ground he fell before it, "your nature intercedes for me and pities me. Assure me that I yet may change these shadows you have shown me by an altered life!"

The kind hand trembled.

"I will honor Christmas in my heart and try to keep it all the year. I will live in the past, the present, and the future. The Spirits of all three shall strive within me. I will not shut out the lessons that they teach. Oh, tell me I may sponge away the writing on this stone!"

In his agony, he caught the spectral hand. It sought to free itself, but he was strong in his entreaty and detained it. The Spirit, stronger yet, repulsed him.

---

[20] Weeds and rank grass kill off all other vegetation.

[21] Dickens is being ironic in so describing a graveyard.

Holding up his hands in one last prayer to have his fate reversed, he saw an alteration in the Phantom's hood and dress. It shrank, collapsed, and dwindled down into a bedpost.

THE END OF IT

Yes! And the bedpost was his own. The bed was his own, the room was his own. Best and happiest of all, the time before him was his own, to make amends in!

"I will live in the past, the present, and the future!" Scrooge repeated as he scrambled out of bed. "The Spirits of all three shall strive within me. O Jacob Marley! Heaven and the Christmastime be praised for this! I say it on my knees, old Jacob, on my knees!"

He was so fluttered and so glowing with his good intentions that his broken voice would scarcely answer to his call. He had been sobbing violently in his conflict with the Spirit, and his face was wet with tears.

"They are not torn down," cried Scrooge, folding one of his bed curtains in his arms. "They are not torn down, rings and all. They are here—I am here— the shadows of the things that would have been may be dispelled. They will be. I know they will!"

His hands were busy with his garments all this time: turning them inside out, putting them on upside down, tearing them, mislaying them, making them parties to every kind of extravagance.

"I don't know what to do!" cried Scrooge, laughing and crying in the same breath and making a perfect Laocoön[1] of himself with his stockings. "I am as

[1] A reference to the famous Roman statue of the fifth century depicting this Trojan priest and his two sons being strangled by serpents. According to Hearn, this was not in the original text, but Dickens, as he was reading the galleys, thought it would be a perfect way to describe Scrooge's contortions with his socks.

light as a feather, I am as happy as an angel, I am as merry as a schoolboy, I am as giddy as a drunken man. A merry Christmas to everybody! A happy New Year to all the world! Hallo here! Whoop! Hallo!"

He had frisked into the sitting room and was now standing there, perfectly winded.

"There's the saucepan that the gruel was in!" cried Scrooge, starting off again and going around the fireplace. "There's the door by which the Ghost of Jacob Marley entered! There's the corner where the Ghost of Christmas Present sat! There's the window where I saw the wandering spirits! It's all right, it's all true, it all happened. Ha, ha, ha!"

Really, for a man who had been out of practice for so many years, it was a splendid laugh, a most illustrious laugh. The father of a long, long line of brilliant laughs!

"I don't know what day of the month it is," said Scrooge. "I don't know how long I have been among the Spirits. I don't know anything. I'm quite a baby. Never mind. I don't care. I'd rather be a baby. Hallo! Whoop! Hallo here!"

He was checked in his transports by the churches ringing out the lustiest peals he had ever heard. Clash, clang, hammer, ding, dong, bell! Bell, dong, ding, hammer, clang, clash! Oh, glorious, glorious!

Running to the window, he opened it and put out his head. No fog, no mist; clear, bright, jovial, stirring, cold; cold, piping for the blood to dance to; golden sunlight; heavenly sky; sweet fresh air; merry bells. Oh, glorious! Glorious!

"What's today?" cried Scrooge, calling downward to a boy in Sunday clothes who perhaps had loitered in to look about him.

"Eh?" returned the boy with all his might of wonder.

"What's today, my fine fellow?" said Scrooge.

"Today!" replied the boy. "Why, CHRISTMAS DAY."

"It's Christmas Day!" said Scrooge to himself. "I haven't missed it. The Spirits have done it all in one night. They can do anything they like. Of course they can. Of course they can. Hallo, my fine fellow!"

"Hallo!" returned the boy.

"Do you know the poulterer's in the next street but one, at the corner?" Scrooge inquired.

"I should hope I did," replied the lad.

"An intelligent boy!" said Scrooge. "A remarkable boy! Do you know whether they've sold the prize turkey that was hanging up there? Not the little prize turkey: the big one?"

"What! The one as big as me?" returned the boy.

"What a delightful boy!" said Scrooge. "It's a pleasure to talk to him. Yes, my buck!"

"It's hanging there now," replied the boy.

"Is it?" said Scrooge. "Go and buy it."

"Walk-ER!"[2] exclaimed the boy.

"No, no," said Scrooge. "I am in earnest. Go and buy it, and tell 'em to bring it here that I may give them the directions where to take it. Come back with the man, and I'll give you a shilling. Come back with him in less than five minutes, and I'll give you half-a-crown!"

The boy was off like a shot. He must have had a steady hand at a trigger who could have got a shot off half as fast.

"I'll send it to Bob Cratchit's," whispered Scrooge, rubbing his hands and splitting with a laugh. "He shan't know who sends it. It's twice the size of Tiny Tim. Joe Miller[3] never made such a joke as sending it to Bob's will be!"

The hand in which he wrote the address was not a steady one; but write it he did, somehow, and went downstairs to open the street door, ready for the coming of the poulterer's man. As he stood there, awaiting his arrival, the knocker caught his eye.

"I shall love it as long as I live!" cried Scrooge, patting it with his hand. "I scarcely ever looked at it before. What an honest expression it has in its face! It's a wonderful knocker! . . . Here's the turkey. Hallo! Whoop! How are you! Merry Christmas!"

It *was* a turkey! He never could have stood upon his legs, that bird. He would have snapped them short off in a minute, like sticks of sealing wax.

"Why, it's impossible to carry that to Camden Town," said Scrooge. "You must have a cab."

The chuckle with which he said this, and the chuckle with which he paid for the turkey, and the chuckle with which he paid for the cab, and the chuckle with which he recompensed the boy, were only to be exceeded by the chuckle with which he sat down, breathless, in his chair again and chuckled till he cried.

Shaving was not an easy task, for his hand continued to shake very much; and shaving requires attention, even when you don't dance while you are at it. But if he had cut the end of his nose off, he would have put a piece of sticking plaster

---

2 A Cockney expression of surprise, incredulity, and sometimes disbelief.

3 A popular but illiterate comic actor (1684–1738). The dramatist John Mottley collected the actor's purported jokes and sayings and published them as *Joe Miller's Jests* (1739), which was—according to Hearn—a jest in itself, as Miller didn't come up with any of them. As a result, almost any joke or jest from then on was attributed to the actor.

over it and been quite satisfied.

He dressed himself "all in his best" and at last got out into the streets. The people were by this time pouring forth, as he had seen them with the Ghost of Christmas Present; and, walking with his hands behind him, Scrooge regarded everyone with a delighted smile. He looked so irresistibly pleasant, in a word, that three or four good-humored fellows said, "Good morning, sir! A merry Christmas to you!" And Scrooge said often afterward that, of all the blithe sounds he had ever heard, those were the blithest in his ears.

He had not gone far when, coming toward him, he beheld the portly gentleman who had walked into his countinghouse the day before and said, "Scrooge and Marley's, I believe?" It sent a pang across his heart to think how this old gentleman would look upon him when they met; but he knew what path lay straight before him, and he took it.

"My dear sir," said Scrooge, quickening his pace and taking the old gentleman by both his hands, "how do you do? I hope you succeeded yesterday. It was very kind of you. A merry Christmas to you, sir!"

"Mr. Scrooge?"

"Yes," said Scrooge. "That is my name, and I fear it may not be pleasant to you. Allow me to ask your pardon. And will you have the goodness—" Here Scrooge whispered in his ear.

"Lord bless me!" cried the gentleman as if his breath were taken away. "My dear Mr. Scrooge, are you serious?"

"If you please," said Scrooge. "Not a farthing less. A great many back payments are included in it, I assure you. Will you do me that favor?"

"My dear sir," said the other, shaking hands with him, "I don't know what to say to such munifi—"

"Don't say anything, please," retorted Scrooge. "Come and see me. Will you come and see me?"

"I will!" cried the old gentleman. And it was clear he meant to do it.

"Thank'ee," said Scrooge. "I am much obliged to you. I thank you fifty times. Bless you!"

He went to church, walked about the streets, watched the people hurrying to and fro, patted the children on the head, questioned beggars, looked down into the kitchens of houses and up to the windows, and found that everything could yield him pleasure. He had never dreamed that any walk—that anything—could give him so much happiness. In the afternoon, he turned his steps toward his nephew's house.

He passed the door a dozen times before he had the courage to go up and

The End of It

knock. But he made a dash and did it.

"Is your master at home, my dear?" said Scrooge to the girl. "Nice girl! Very."

"Yes, sir."

"Where is he, my love?" said Scrooge.

"He's in the dining room, along with the mistress. I'll show you upstairs, if you please."

"Thank'ee. He knows me," said Scrooge with his hand already on the dining-room lock. "I'll go in here, my dear."

He turned it gently and sidled his face in around the door. They were looking at the table (which was spread out in great array); for these young housekeepers are always nervous on such points and like to see that everything is right.

"Fred!" said Scrooge.

Dear heart alive, how his niece by marriage started! Scrooge had forgotten, for the moment, about her sitting in the corner with the footstool, or he wouldn't have done it on any account.

"Why, bless my soul!" cried Fred. "Who's that?"

"It's I. Your uncle Scrooge. I have come to dinner. Will you let me in, Fred?"

Let him in! It is a mercy he didn't shake his arm off. He was "at home" in five minutes. Nothing could be heartier. His niece looked just the same. So did Topper when *he* came. So did the plump sister when *she* came. So did everyone when *they* came. Wonderful party, wonderful games, wonderful unanimity, won-der-ful happiness!

But he was early at the office the next morning.[4] Oh, he was early there! If he could only be there first and catch Bob Cratchit coming late! That was the thing he had set his heart upon.

And he did it; yes, he did! The clock struck nine. No Bob. A quarter past. No Bob. He was a full eighteen minutes and a half behind his time. Scrooge sat with his door wide open that he might see him come into the tank.

His hat was off before he opened the door; his scarf, too. He was on his stool in a jiffy, driving away with his pen, as if he were trying to overtake nine o'clock.

"Hallo!" growled Scrooge in his accustomed voice, as near as he could feign it. "What do you mean by coming here at this time of day?"

"I am very sorry, sir," said Bob. "I *am* behind my time."

"You are!" repeated Scrooge. "Yes, I think you are. Step this way, sir, if you please."

---

[4] St. Stephen's Day (Boxing Day), when gifts were normally given to those who had provided services during the year.

"It's only once a year, sir," pleaded Bob, appearing from the tank. "It shall not be repeated. I was making rather merry yesterday, sir."

"Now, I'll tell you what, my friend," said Scrooge. "I am not going to stand this sort of thing any longer. And therefore—" He leaped from his stool and gave Bob such a dig in the waistcoat that he staggered back into the tank again. "And therefore I am about to raise your salary!"

Bob trembled and got a little nearer to the ruler. He had a momentary idea of knocking Scrooge down with it, holding him, and calling to the people in the court for help and a straitjacket.

"A merry Christmas, Bob!" said Scrooge with an earnestness that could not be mistaken; he clapped him on the back. "A merrier Christmas, Bob, my good fellow, than I have given you for many a year! I'll raise your salary and endeavor to assist your struggling family. We will discuss your affairs this very afternoon over a Christmas bowl of smoking bishop, Bob! Make up the fires and buy another coal scuttle before you dot another 'i,' Bob Cratchit!"

Scrooge was better than his word. He did it all and infinitely more; and to Tiny Tim, who did NOT die, he was a second father. He became as good a friend, as good a master, and as good a man as the good old city knew, or any other good old city, town, or borough in the good old world. Some people laughed to see the alteration in him, but he let them laugh and little heeded them; for he was wise enough to know that nothing ever happened on this globe for good at which some people did not have their fill of laughter in the outset; and knowing that such as these would be blind anyway, he thought it quite as well that they should wrinkle up their eyes in grins as have the malady in less attractive forms. His own heart laughed, and that was quite enough for him.

He had no further intercourse with Spirits, but lived upon the Total Abstinence Principle[5] ever afterward—and it was always said of him that he knew how to keep Christmas well, if any man alive possessed the knowledge. May that be truly said of us, and all of us! And so, as Tiny Tim observed: *God Bless Us, Every One!*

---

[5] The abstinence from alcohol spirits is used here by Dickens as a pun in referring to supernatural ones.

DISCUSSION WITH
PROFESSOR WHEELER
(For Formal School, Home School, and Book Club Discussions)

First of all, permit me to define my perception of the role of the teacher. I believe that the ideal teaching relationship involves the teacher and the student, both looking in the same direction, and both with a sense of wonder. A teacher is not an important person dishing out rote learning to an unimportant person. I furthermore do not believe that a Ph.D. automatically brings with it omniscience, despite the way some of us act. In discussions, I tell my students beforehand that my opinions and conclusions are no more valid than theirs, for each of us sees reality from a different perspective.

Now that my role is clear, let's continue. The purpose of the discussion section of the series is to encourage debate, to dig deeper into the books than would be true without it, and to spawn other questions that may build on the ones I begin with here. If you take advantage of this section, you will be gaining just as good an understanding of the book as you would were you actually sitting in one of my classroom circles.

As you read this book, record your thoughts and reactions each day in a journal. Also, an unabridged dictionary is almost essential in completely understanding the text. If your vocabulary is to grow, something else is needed besides the dictionary: vocabulary cards. Take a stack of 3x5 cards, and write the words you don't know on one side and their definitions on the other, with each word used in a sentence. Every time you stumble on words you are unsure of—and I found quite a number myself!—make a card for it. Continually go over these cards; and keep all, except those you never miss, in a card file. You will be amazed at how fast your vocabulary will grow!

The Introduction Must Be Read Before
Beginning Next Section

QUESTIONS TO DEEPEN YOUR UNDERSTANDING

Stave One: Marley's Ghost

1. The statement "Scrooge's name was good upon the Exchange" means that while Scrooge may have been stingy and bitter, he was perceived as being ethical. His name stood for something. In Dickens's day, one's name meant a great deal. Dishonoring it dishonored the entire family and was perceived as being worse than death itself. If one's father or mother died with unpaid debts—even if that person had declared bankruptcy—the surviving children felt an obligation to repay every penny.

    Today, honor is an attribute to which we pay little attention. Listen to any TV talk show and you will hear individuals "telling all" just to gain notice, notoriety, and money.

    And, worse yet, our legal system has encouraged us to believe that if something is legal that means it must also be right. Is that always true? Give some examples.

    Discuss what it means to "have a good name," to be considered trustworthy and dependable, to have bankers declare that your word is all the security they need. What has been lost since the time a person's word and handshake were enough to seal a contract? How is our society different today? Why do you think things have changed?

2. Scrooge is the ultimate miser. We learn in Scripture and in life that God has a way of balancing out what we do and say. In other words, the way we treat others is how we'll be treated—usually compounded. One does not have to believe in God for this principle to be operative: Sooner or later, life comes full circle.

    Scrooge, during the course of this drama, discovers that truth. The Third Spirit graphically reveals the tragic results of a self-centered life.

Each time you come across a statement in the book that has to do with generosity, giving, service to others, write it down; then, at the end, compare them and arrive at conclusions. Finally, discuss what lessons you feel Dickens intended us to gain from the story.

3. Dickens implies that each of us carries our own "weather" with us. Do you feel that is true? If so, what can we do about it in our own interactions with people?

4. Scrooge's nephew plays a significant role in the story. Note that he does not weary of doing good: Every Christmas, he wishes his crusty uncle a merry Christmas and invites him home to share the holiday with his family. Eventually, when Scrooge's heart is softened, these persistent attempts to be friendly and kind bear fruit.

What does this say to us in terms of our interactions with others? How should we behave toward those who do not respond kindly or graciously toward our overtures of friendship? Is there ever a situation in which a person should not be treated with kindness and respect? Explain.

Is it possible that too many of us demand instant gratification? Are we unwilling for God to take our kind words and acts and use them to gradually break down walls of resistance? What should we do about it?

5. Is it true, as Fred maintains, that people tend to treat each other differently during the Christmas season? If it is true, give some examples of how people, including ourselves, do this. Is that a good thing or a bad thing? Should we treat people the "Christmas way" all year round? Why?

6. The two gentlemen who ask Scrooge to donate to the poor play a key role in the book. Explain what that role is, and how it affects Scrooge. Discuss the role of giving, of tithing, in our lives. Should there be guidelines?

Should we first research an organization before we give (to see if they are illegitimate or top-heavy—in other words, with a disproportionate percentage of the money raised used for management overhead rather than for the ostensible cause)? Is that good stewardship? What is stewardship?

7. Does supporting established charities mean we no longer need to give in cases of individual need? We've all been approached, from time to time, by panhandlers—people we are certain will use the requested "food" money for liquor, drugs, or tobacco. How should we respond?

I make it a policy to never turn anyone down completely—I will always give something. Even when I am almost certain it will be misused. The important thing is to respond to the request with both love and respect, remembering that Christ would have died for the person asking for help. In every interaction I have, from day to day, I try to remember to be kind to each of our Lord's sheep.

Discuss, at length, the exciting and challenging issue of philanthropy.

8. Scrooge refers to the poor and needy as the "surplus population." Like Scrooge, certain groups in our society believe overpopulation will eventually destroy our planet if something isn't done to control the birth rate. Is there a golden mean? Explain.

9. Do we sometimes act like ostriches, sticking our heads in the sand to avoid seeing others' needs? Do we say, in effect, "As long as I don't know for sure what's going on, I'm not accountable for following through and helping out"? If so, what should we do about it?

10. Scrooge pays Cratchit as little as possible. For that, we scorn Scrooge. Later on, when Scrooge becomes generous, we praise him. Having said that, why is it that so many professed Christians are perceived to be such tightwads when it comes to being generous with their employees? One would think that, of all people,

Christians would be the most generous! What can we do to correct this tendency/perspective?

11. In the story, Dickens repeatedly comes back to accountability: the concept that each of us, like it or not, is our brother's keeper; that, if we walk through life thinking only of ourselves, it will be virtually impossible for us to be happy or feel blessed. Discuss.

12. Marley tells Scrooge that, as a result of each day's acts and words, we forge links in a chain that we must drag around with us for eternity after we die. C. S. Lewis, in that monumental little book *Mere Christianity,* puts it a little differently. He points out that each decision, act, conversation, and so on, makes a "mark on the soul." Singly, these marks are not very significant, but over time they tend to cluster, and these clusters become habits, and habits evolve into character, and character eventually determines one's eternal destiny.

Compare the two metaphors in terms of the impact on the choices we make every moment of our lives, keeping in mind the truth that, every day, either we are moving toward being nobler creatures who are more in tune with the divine, or we are going in the opposite direction.

13. One of the most powerful quotations in the book is this one:
" 'Business!' " cried the Ghost, wringing its hands again.
" 'Mankind was my business. The common welfare was my business; charity, mercy, forbearance, and benevolence were all my business. The details of my trade were but a drop of water in the comprehensive ocean of my business.' "

Think about what Marley says here: Basically, we could establish an international corporation and become a household name; yet if we aren't being our brother's keeper on a daily basis, our success and fame avail us nothing. Do you think that's true? Why, or why not?

If that concept is true, what is Dickens saying to us about our priorities, especially our tendency to equate success with money and possessions rather than with qualities of the heart? Discuss.

Stave Two: The First of the Three Spirits

14. When Scrooge reexperiences his past, for the first time we note good qualities in him. Dickens himself, in writing *Carol,* was using his own past as a way of arriving at the truth about himself. How important is it that we periodically journey back to our past experiences? What should we look for there? To what kind of past experiences does the Second Ghost take Scrooge? What would be our own counterparts to them?

15. Discuss this strange paradox: Scrooge strongly resists leaving his past once he gets there—almost as strongly as he resisted remembering the past in the first place! Only after vicariously reexperiencing the kindness he received from others when he was young does Scrooge see how inhumanely he treats people now. Looking at it from a different angle: It was not verbal sermons that changed his heart; it was physical sermons, represented by kind acts, that made the difference. We impact others by the lives we lead, not merely by the words we speak.

16. In his biography in the introduction, Dickens, in rediscovering his childhood self, also rediscovers how much books meant to him as a child. Discuss how much is lost in life by the failure to fall in love with good books. How much is lost in the mind by failure to grow in our reading? How much do we cripple our potential in life by failing to read good books?

17. Perhaps the saddest words in this story are these: "It's too late now." For most of us, these words are likely to come to mind when we are at the funerals of friends and loved ones, as we realize that the kind words we might have said, the kind things we might have done, are all moot now: no more useful to us than the three-day banknote Scrooge worries about on the fourth day.

Kalidasa, one of India's greatest poets, addressed that human problem in a 1,500-year-old poem called "Salutation to the

Dawn." It is a poem that had a major impact on my life years ago and continues to have today. At my urging, many of my students have memorized it, and many since then have told me it has changed their lives.

The essence of Kalidasa's message is this: Every day is in itself a miniature lifetime, with a beginning, a middle, and an end. Energy devoted to yesterday and tomorrow is energy wasted, for regret and worry are futile. Only as we concentrate on today, the one time-frame we can do anything about, can we make a success of our lives. The beauty of the message is this: Once we are able to hold our heads high and face God with our todays, saying, "Lord, if you were to judge my life by today, I would be content, for I've tried to be a good steward, I've tried to use wisely the time you've entrusted to me, I've tried to grow, and I've tried to minister to those sheep of Yours that I came into contact with today," will we be able to cease regretting yesterday and worrying about tomorrow.

Since this poem ties in so perfectly with *A Christmas Carol,* I am including it in its entirety, for you to memorize, assimilate, and live by:

Salutation to the Dawn

> Look to this day!
> For it is life, the very life of life.
> In its brief course
> Lie all the verities and realities of your
>   existence—
> The bliss of growth,
> The glory of action,
> The splendor of achievement.
> For yesterday is already a dream
> And tomorrow is only a vision,
> But today well lived
> Makes every yesterday a dream of happiness
> And every tomorrow a vision of hope.
> Look well, therefore, to this day!
> Such is the salutation to the dawn.

Discuss the significance of the concepts in the poem.

18. In reliving his sister Fan's kindness again, in retrospect, Scrooge sees his own self-centeredness in a new light—again, by contrast. Too often we ignore the love and kindness expressed, from day to day, in our own families. What can we do about it?

19. The scene with Fezziwig vividly brings home to Scrooge the fact that he has been a terrible boss to Cratchit. Scrooge experiences something else at Fezziwig's that he had lost: the ability to carpe diem (seize the day)—to gain joy out of every nuance, every moment, of every day; hence, the changed life in the fifth stave (what, in King James language is termed "the abundant life"). How incredible that Christians, of all people, should walk around morosely, as if there were no God and the world had caved in on them! Discuss.

20. In reexperiencing his own broken engagement, Scrooge realizes how much he has lost in throwing away Belle's love. "And for what?" he now asks himself. Scrooge realizes that there was a price to pay for his being too busy and too selfish to marry and have children: a lonely old age.

Discuss the roles of marriage, family, and children in our lives.

Stave Three: The Second of the Three Spirits

21. If there is one word that capsulizes this book, it is kindness, one of the most crucial and far-reaching qualities in God's universe. Without it, life is sad and miserable, both for the person who fails to practice the quality and for those who come into contact with that person. From the story, discuss instances of the presence or absence of kindness, and the difference it makes. Note that the Second Ghost sprinkles that "gift" on people passing by.

22. What does the Cratchit scene accomplish in the book? How—and why—does Scrooge change as he watches them celebrate Christmas together? Who in the family softens Scrooge's heart the most? Why? What are the lessons we can gain from that truth?

23. At Fred's house, the people are having a rollicking good time. How is Scrooge changed by what he sees and hears? What causes these changes? What should be the significance to us? For instance, what should be the role of play in our lives?

Stave Four: The Last of the Spirits

24. This stave is, by far, the most devastating of all. All the action leads into it, and Scrooge must at last face his moment of truth. Note how Dickens pulls it off: Rather than telling about Scrooge's demise through passive narration, he drops the reader into separate, apparently unrelated, conversations with people on the street. One has the feeling of actually being there, listening in, and having to pull the information together oneself.

Discuss this aspect of writing—that is, letting dialogue, rather than narration, carry the story. What does each of these conversations contribute to the whole? Study each one carefully, and compare.

25. Note how Dickens is a master at being able to arrive at the personality essence of an individual by just honing in on dialogue. Study each character in the book, even those who are only given a few lines; then see if you can construct a core of individuality out of that. In our own writing, how can we learn from Dickens in this respect?

26. As the stave progresses, how does Dickens orchestrate increasing horror on the part of Scrooge?

27. What is accomplished by the return to the Cratchit family?

28. What is accomplished by the fact that the Third Ghost is mute—says not a word?

29. Starting with the Third Ghost, analyze the role of each ghost in the overall scheme of the book. How is each one different? What does each contribute to the whole?

Stave Five: The End of It

30. Describe (starting from the first stave and moving toward the end) how Scrooge changes during the course of the story. What causes the biggest changes? Do they occur all at once or gradually? After doing that, compile two character studies: Scrooge at the beginning, and Scrooge at the end. Compare them. Do you feel the changes are justified by the action and the dialogue? Explain.

31. Discuss the impact of the story. What was the overall effect on you? Do you feel this effect will be short-lived? Or do you feel it will affect the way you treat others for a long time? Explain and discuss.

CODA

Reactions, responses, and suggestions are very important to us. Also, if a particular book—especially an older one—has been loved by you or your family, and you would like to see us incorporate it into this series, drop us a line, with details you know about its earliest publisher, printing date, and so on, and send it to

Joe Wheeler, Ph.D.
c/o Focus on the Family
Colorado Springs, CO 80920

ABOUT THE EDITOR

Joseph Leininger Wheeler's earliest memories have to do with books and stories—more specifically, of listening to his mother read aloud both in public and to him at home. Wheeler recalls that, as soon as he was able to read, he followed his mother around the house, relentlessly reading his storybooks to her.

Shortly after Wheeler turned eight, his parents moved from California to Latin America as missionaries. From the third through the tenth grade, he was home-schooled by his mother. Of those years, he says today, "I was incredibly lucky and blessed. My mother, a trained teacher and elocutionist, was a voracious reader of books worth reading and had memorized thousands of pages of readings, poetry, and stories. All of that she poured into me. Wherever we went, she encouraged me to devour entire libraries."

At 16, Wheeler returned to California to complete his high school years at Monterey Bay Academy near Santa Cruz. Because of his inherited love of the printed word, Wheeler majored in history at Pacific Union College in the Napa Valley, completing both bachelor's and master's degrees there. After completing a master's in English at California State University in Sacramento, Wheeler attended Vanderbilt University, where he obtained a Ph.D. in English.

Today, after 34 years of teaching at the adult education, college, high school, and junior high levels, Wheeler is Professor Emeritus at Columbia Union College in Takoma Park, Maryland. The world's foremost authority on frontier writer Zane Grey, Wheeler is also the founder and executive director of Zane Grey's West Society and Senior Fellow for Cultural Studies at the Center for the New West in Denver, Colorado. He is editor/compiler of the popular *Christmas in My Heart* series (Review & Herald; Doubleday, Dell, Bantam); editor/compiler of the story anthologies *Dad in My Heart* and *Mom in My Heart* (Tyndale House); and editor/compiler of the *Great Stories Remembered* and Classic Collection series for Focus on the Family. Along the way, Wheeler has established nine libraries in schools and colleges, as well as building up his own collection (as large as some college libraries).

Joe Wheeler and his wife, Connie, are the parents of two grown children, Greg and Michelle, and now make their home in Conifer, Colorado.